Somehow she was in his heart now as much
as the sea itself.

His han...
and he...
wanted...
his arm...
came u...
gathering storm.

He heard Chloe give a soft gasp, but she
didn't resist. What he saw reflected back in

Also by Susan Carroll
Published by Fawcett Books:

THE LADY WHO HATED SHAKESPEARE
THE SUGAR ROSE
BRIGHTON ROAD
THE BISHOP'S DAUGHTER
THE WOOING OF MISS MASTERS

CHRISTMAS BELLES

Susan Carroll

FAWCETT CREST • NEW YORK

A Fawcett Crest Book
Published by Ballantine Books
Copyright © 1992 by Susan Coppula

All rights reserved under International and Pan-American Copyright Conventions. Published in the United States by Ballantine Books, a division of Random House, Inc., New York, and simultaneously in Canada by Random House of Canada Limited, Toronto.

Library of Congress Catalog Card Number: 92-90597

ISBN 0-449-21953-4

Manufactured in the United States of America

First Edition: November 1992

To four of my most devoted fans: Dorothy, Pat, Jean, and Janet—who, by pure coincidence, also happen to be my sisters.

Prologue

Christmas Eve, 1805

Never had sprigs of mistletoe been nailed into place with such fierce determination. Miss Chloe Anne Waverly balanced atop the ladder, smacking her hammer against the nail, her blue eyes squinting at the clang of every blow. Her slender frame swayed precariously, her shimmering lengths of honey brown hair tumbling across the delicate contours of her face. Pursing her lips, she dealt the stubborn nail another mighty wham.

"Chloe Anne!" Her older sister's voice rang out sharply. "Do finish with that before you break your neck or my ears. The infernal racket you are making! It goes quite through my head."

Using the handle of the hammer, Chloe brushed the hair back from her eyes and glanced down to where Lucy stood on the other side of the arched doorway that led into the parlor. The neat arrangement of Lucy's blond ringlets made Chloe more conscious of her own disheveled state. But then, she had never seen Lucy look anything less than what she aspired to be: a young lady of high fashion and elegance, from her soft leather pattens to her immaculately manicured fingertips.

Lucy took great care that the folds of her soft

kerseymere gown did not snag against the ladder. Even her slight frown in nowise diminished her beauty.

"When you said you intended to hang the mistletoe," Lucy complained, "I did not know you meant to kill it. Surely you can find some more merciful means of execution."

"I've nearly finished. You want me to make a proper job of it, don't you?" Chloe asked, making a sweeping gesture with the hammer. She always talked with her hands. She could not seem to help it. "It wouldn't do to have the kissing bough come tumbling down in the midst of our celebrations."

Lucy took a step back, warily eyeing the movements of the hammer. "I scarce see what difference it makes. Who do you fancy there will be to kiss? Only Papa or old Squire Daniels, whose breath always smells like tobacco and onions."

"You can never tell." Chloe dreamily regarded the bough of dark green leaves with its pallid berries. "Perchance we might have some unexpected visitor."

"And perchance we won't."

"But we could—someone young and handsome."

"But we won't." Lucy smiled sweetly and stalked away.

"But we *might*," Chloe muttered under her breath. She tightened her grip upon the hammer, but she could not help pausing to watch as Lucy rustled gracefully past the settee, where their youngest sister, Agnes, reclined, deeply engrossed in a book.

Chloe had a deep and abiding appreciation of all that was beautiful, and Lucy was certainly that. If her own eyes were blue, Lucy's were bluer. Her hair had tints of sunlight, but Lucy's was spun gold. She was short, but Lucy was tall and statuesque.

And although she was only a year older than Chloe, Lucy had a bosom.

Ruefully, Chloe stole a furtive glance down the front of her high-waisted frock. She had just turned sixteen last month and was still as flat-chested as Dan, the stableboy.

Ah, well. Someday, she thought with a tiny sigh. Chloe was a great believer in all good things coming to those who waited long enough. Cheerfully, she resumed her hammering until she was certain that the bough of mistletoe was there to stay. Then she carefully ascended the ladder to survey her handiwork.

Besides the mistletoe in the arch, she had decorated the parlor as well with swags of holly draped about the mantel, evergreen festooned in loops over the windows. The mullioned panes sparkled with a crystal sheen of frost. A roaring fire had been banked upon the hearth, and although the night wind sang past the shutters, the parlor seemed snug and cozy.

Chloe Anne could already feel it, a kind of magic that quickened her blood, that special magic that came only on Christmas Eve, as hushed as a new-fallen blanket of snow, as warm and glowing as a candle's flame. The magic seemed to have transformed the parlor until one quite forgot the shabbiness of the carpet, the settee pillows turned over to disguise the fact that the velvet had faded. Not that Chloe noticed those things anyway, except when Lucy pointed them out to her.

Her decorating finished, Chloe found herself with nothing to do but take a restless turn about the parlor. Tingles of excitement and happy anticipation coursed through her, and she wished she had someone to share the feeling with. But Lucy sat at the parlor table, absorbed in examining the largess of her presents, and Agnes never looked up from her book.

The girl was reading *Homer*, not the Chapman translation, but in the original Greek. Agnes was so clever, it was almost alarming.

After regarding her sisters' preoccupation in wistful silence, Chloe Anne clapped her hands together in hearty fashion and rubbed them briskly. "Oh, do let us go for a walk or something. We could go down by the old oak and see if the Christmas rose has begun to bloom."

"In the cold and dark?" Lucy's brow arched with incredulity.

Agnes raised her sharp little nose up from her book long enough to comment. "It isn't properly a rose plant at all, only a species of hellebore."

"But it's called a Christmas rose because it blooms at Christmas," Chloe said.

"That's only a legend. There is no reason it should bloom on Christmas rather than any other day of winter. Plants cannot read the almanac." Agnes's look was as severe as that of the sternest old governess. Sometimes, Chloe thought with vexed amusement, her younger sister seemed more like fourteen going on forty.

"It would do you no harm to go for a walk anyway, Agnes," Lucy chimed in. "You spend too much time at your studies. You are going to end up with great bumps over your eyes."

"It is far better than what you do, constantly primping in front of a mirror. You have wasted your entire evening gloating over that pile of fripperies."

4

Lucy flushed and circled one arm rather protectively around her newly acquired collection of fans, gloves, and jars of scent. "You need not be so spiteful merely because I received more presents than you. If you had been invited to visit Cousin Harriet in London, you would never have made as many kind friends as I did, for you never take the pains to be agreeable to anyone."

"I would not want such friends or such a heap of rubbish." Grumpily, Agnes nestled deeper against the settee cushions, subsiding once more into her book.

Lucy turned her eyes to Chloe, looking half-defiant, half-ashamed. "I feel quite badly that the rest of you have not received so much. Of course, I . . ." She hesitated and took a deep swallow. "I intend to share."

"Why, Lucy, that is very generous of you." Chloe Anne schooled her jaw not to drop open. It was generous of Lucy and decidedly unusual. Sharing had never come easily to her lovely sister. But, unlike Agnes, Chloe did not grudge Lucy her store of treasures or her visits to London. In fact, Chloe feared the sojourns had done Lucy little good, merely providing her with tantalizing glimpses of a glittering, fashionable world in which she, as the daughter of an impoverished knight, could not hope to take part. It left Lucy more discontented than ever with the simple life they led at Windhaven Manor, isolated along a sweep of coast in Norfolk.

Chloe Anne made haste to assure Lucy that she did not feel any of the fans would suit her, nor did she really care for that brand of scent.

"Well, if you are really sure . . ." Lucy said with a regretful smile, but her sigh was tinged with relief. She was just beginning to scoop her treasured hoard from the table when Emma entered the room. At the age of twenty, Emma was the eldest of the Waverly girls.

Chloe Anne pounced upon her sister at once, eager for someone to share her enthusiasm. She dragged Emma about the parlor, calling upon her to admire the decorations.

Emma wiped her hands on the folds of her apron, a few wisps of soft brown hair escaping her chignon to frame her plump, pretty face. She summoned up a placid smile.

"It is all very pleasant, dear," Emma said.

"Pleasant," Chloe Anne echoed drearily. She was fond of all her sisters in different ways. But sometimes she felt like giving them each a sharp poke with a pin. At least that might produce some small shriek of excitement from them. She supposed she might as well resign herself. She could expect no real enthusiasm until Papa came home from calling at the vicarage. Papa was the only one who ever seemed to throw himself into the festivities with the same unbridled delight as she did.

Emma gave Chloe Anne a motherly pat on the shoulder. "I am sure we shall have a very nice Christmas. I have just been checking on the plum pudding. Even though it is my first effort at such a thing, I believe it may be the best dinner we've ever had."

Lucy groaned. "There is no need for you to go announcing that to anyone else, Em."

"Oh, Lord, no," Agnes piped up scornfully. "The world mustn't know we are so unrefined that we *eat*."

"Not that we eat," Lucy snapped. "That we cook."

6

"*We*, dearest?" Emma laughed with one of her rare flashes of humor.

Lucy pulled a face but could not refrain from smiling a little at herself. It was a well-known fact that Lucy never went near the kitchens except to demand more hot water for her bath. But they did not have as many indoor servants these days at Windhaven, only Polly, the maid, and Old Meg, the cook. Emma, being of a domestic turn, had taken to helping out with the preparation of meals. Chloe had also tried to do her share, but being a little too inclined to daydream, she was something of a disaster in the kitchens. Ever since the day she burned the bread so hard and black it could have been used to repair the crumbling stone at the north end of the house, Old Meg had threatened Chloe with the soup ladle if she "durst cross the threshold of my kitchen again."

Chloe had felt both guilty and relieved at the ban. It seemed unfair that the burden of maintaining the household should fall on Emma's shoulders. Yet she never complained, not even at times like this evening, when she was looking a little tired.

Forcing Agnes to draw in her feet, Chloe gave Emma a gentle nudge until she plunked down beside the younger girl on the settee. Emma flashed her a grateful smile, then mopped her forehead with the heel of her hand.

"I declare, it seems hotter in here than it was in the kitchen. How much wood you girls have stacked upon that fire. We won't even need the Yule log brought in."

"That's Chloe Anne's doing," Lucy said. "She's been brewing some sort of concoction in that little black pot."

Agnes turned another page of her book and

7

sniffed. "Probably some other beastly old Christmas custom she has discovered and means to inflict upon all of us."

"It has nothing to do with Christmas," Chloe Anne said. "Or at least only a little bit." She had nearly forgotten about the little iron pot she had suspended over the hottest part of the flames. But now she hastened over to check its contents.

"Actually, what I have been doing," she told her sisters, "is melting some of Papa's lead shot."

This announcement at least produced some reaction from them. The parlor chorused with their exclamations.

"What!"

"Melting lead?"

"Whatever for?"

"Another of Chloe's half-mad schemes," Agnes said. "You may depend upon it."

Chloe Anne smiled sheepishly. "Perhaps it is a little mad. But I was talking to the squire's housekeeper, Mrs. Brindle. She told me of the most interesting old legend—"

Her sisters united in a heartfelt groan.

"No, do but listen," Chloe insisted. "Mrs. Brindle told me that if an unmarried girl drops molten lead into cold water on Christmas Eve, the lead will assume a shape, give her some sign of what her future husband will be."

"What next!" Lucy exclaimed. "Now the girl is passing the time of day with housekeepers. Have you no sense of decorum, Chloe Anne?"

"It is all utter nonsense anyway," Agnes added. "Wait until Papa hears how you have been wasting his lead shot."

"Papa won't care," Chloe said. "I do not believe he has ever shot anything in his life, not even a

8

rabbit. Oh, please," she said coaxingly. "Let us just try dropping the lead in water. What harm can it do? It is only a bit of fun."

Agnes merely snorted with disgust, and Lucy rolled her eyes. But Emma, as ever willing to indulge Chloe Anne, joined her at the fireside, though Chloe Anne suspected her sister came as much to insure that Chloe did not burn herself as for any other reason.

Whatever Emma's motives, both she and Chloe crowded round a bucket of cold water. Chloe carefully dipped up a ladle full of lead and tipped it into the bucket. The molten lead hit the water with an awful hiss and a cloud of steam. Chloe waved her hand, trying to disperse the haze before her eyes.

When the shape in the water became visible, Emma said, "I fear it doesn't look like much of anything to me."

That didn't surprise Chloe. When she pointed to clouds overhead, indicating the shapes of horses, daffodils, dancing cats, Emma never saw those either.

Chloe narrowed her eyes, applying her own powers of perception to the lead solidifying in the water. "It looks like a cross of some sort. That must mean that your husband will be a . . . a religious man, a man of the cloth, perhaps."

"Oh!" was all that Emma said, but a peculiar look crossed her face. Her cheeks turned bright pink with a most self-conscious expression.

For all her feigned sophistication and amusement at the proceedings, Lucy also crowded close to peer into the bucket.

"Do mine next," she demanded.

Chloe Anne obeyed. After another hiss from the bucket, she studied the forming shape.

"It looks like a lump of something," she said.

"A lump of lead. Only a lump of lead," Agnes was heard to mutter from her post on the settee.

"No, a lump of gold!" Chloe cried triumphantly. "The fates proclaim that Lucy is to marry a very wealthy man."

Lucy giggled. "Tell the fates I am much obliged to them. And could he have a title as well?"

While she, Emma, and Chloe laughed at their own nonsense, Agnes shook her head darkly. "Candidates for Bedlam, the lot of you."

She resisted all attempts to coax her to join in the game. When Lucy went so far as playfully trying to drag her from the settee, Agnes dealt her hand a ringing slap.

Lucy rubbed her stinging knuckles, but she still chuckled. "All right for you, Madam Sourpuss. Let us do yours, then, Chloe Anne."

Nodding, Chloe raised up the ladle for the last time. She told herself that it was only a silly game, all in fun, but that did not prevent her hand from trembling a little as she poured the lead. She watched for the shape forming in the water, her heart thudding with eager anticipation.

Her excitement quickly turned to puzzlement. She squinted at the scrap of lead. "It . . . it looks like an arrow."

"I suppose that means you are going to marry Robin of the Hood," Agnes called out derisively.

"No, it might not be an arrow," Lucy said. "It's more of a sword or dagger."

Emma smiled. "Perhaps that means you are going to marry a soldier."

"Oh!" Chloe exclaimed. "I shouldn't like that. I would not want a soldier for my husband."

"What about a sailor, then?" a jolly voice boomed from the doorway.

Chloe turned sharply at the same time as her sisters to regard the stout, elderly gentleman who stood framed beneath the arch.

"Papa!"

Sir Phineas Waverly paused to blow on his palms, his hands chafed raw from the cold. He had forgotten to wear his gloves again, likewise his hat. The ends of his graying hair straggled across his brow, his side-whiskers badly in need of a trim. Even though the hem on the cape of his caped coat was slightly frayed, in Chloe Anne's eyes, he still cut quite the dashing figure, very much what he must have been on that glorious long-ago day he had been named a Knight of the Bath.

As he shed his cloak, he looked about him, saying, "How well the decorations look, my dears. But bless me, you've forgotten the mistletoe."

It was a game of Papa's since the days of their childhood. Sir Phineas always stood directly beneath the kissing bough, pretending to be ignorant of its existence until he should be captured.

"Oh, Papa." Agnes groaned. "We are far too old for such jesting."

But Chloe Anne was already rushing forward, with Emma not far behind. Lucy for once forgot her newly acquired sophistication and romped with the rest. While Chloe launched a frontal attack, Emma and Lucy moved in from the sides, surrounding Sir Phineas, covering his bewhiskered cheeks with ruthless kisses. He struggled manfully, but as his defense took the form of seizing each girl in a great bear hug, his protestations were not taken seriously.

Agnes was at last driven to abandon her book

and join them, giving her father a prim peck on the cheek. Not, she was at great pains to assure everyone, because it had anything to do with the mistletoe. No, she always greeted her father thus when he returned from a long absence.

"Indeed," Lucy mocked. "Papa must have been gone all of three hours."

Agnes glared at her.

"More like five," Chloe corrected. She regarded her father reproachfully. "You have been at the vicarage forever, Papa. You were not even here to hang the holly."

"It could not be helped, my dear." Sir Phineas exhaled a deep sigh. The glow that had suffused through him from all the hearty embracing seemed to fade. He crossed the room to hold out his hands to the roaring blaze. "Ah, that feels better."

While Emma scolded Papa for forgetting his gloves, Chloe Anne surreptitiously sought to remove the bucket of water. Not that she feared Papa would be angry over the waste of shot, but he was bound to ask the nature of the game, and Chloe did not want to explain. Papa would laugh at such nonsense, but he would look rather sad as well. He always did at any talk of husbands for them. Chloe was fully aware how much her father had worried of late about the difficulty of providing suitable portions for his daughters.

Was it such worries that troubled him even tonight, Christmas Eve? For Papa was troubled about something. The more Chloe observed him, the more she was sure of it. Despite the pockets of age beneath Papa's eyes, the eyes themselves retained the glow of youth, as bright as any candle flame. But tonight not even the reflection of fire shine brought any sparkle to his eyes.

"Papa," Chloe asked rather anxiously, "was all well at the vicarage?"

Sir Phineas's brow was knit in abstraction, and Chloe had to repeat the question before she gained his attention.

"What? Oh yes, quite well. In fact, I invited Mr. Henry to come dine with us this evening, help drag the Yule log in."

"Did you, Papa? How splendid," Chloe said.

The vicar of St. Andrew's Church was a pleasant young man, shy and a little too solemn, perhaps, but very earnest, eager to please. He was new to their parish and having a difficult time of it, as the previous incumbent, poor Mr. Bledsoe, held the living for some sixty-odd years. Squire Daniels was heard to remark loudly every Sunday that he was having difficulty becoming accustomed to being preached at by some cub not even old enough to shave.

Chloe had indignantly told him that she was perfectly sure Mr. Henry did shave, perhaps as much as thrice a day, but that had only made the old squire roar with laughter. With Mr. Henry having a hard time gaining acceptance hereabouts, Chloe was pleased that Papa had been kind enough to think of the young man on Christmas Eve.

Lucy received the news of Mr. Henry's inclusion in their party with indifference, and Agnes merely turned another page of her book. Chloe thought Emma would be as pleased as she, but her older sister had fallen unusually silent.

Chloe could not refrain from remarking triumphantly to Lucy, "There! Did I not tell you when I was hanging the mistletoe that we might have another visitor besides the squire. Someone young and handsome."

"Young, perhaps," Lucy said with a lift of her brow. "But certainly not handsome. Mr. Henry's chin is too pointed."

"And he is thin as a broomstick," Agnes murmured from behind her book.

Emma shot to her feet. "I do not see anything wrong with Mr. Henry's chin, and he might not be so thin if—if he had someone to properly look after him."

Chloe and the others only stared at her. It was rare to hear Emma speak so sharply. Looking considerably flustered, she excused herself, declaring matters in the kitchen warranted her attention, and bolted from the room.

"Well! Whatever got into her?" Lucy asked.

"Probably worried that there won't be enough pudding to go around," was Agnes's conjecture.

Emma might have been disconcerted at the prospect of providing for an extra guest, but Chloe did not think so. She had never seen her serene elder sister behave so oddly, nor Papa either. His air of melancholy only seemed to increase after Emma's withdrawal. But when he caught Chloe staring at him, he was quick to smile and shake off the mood.

He paced about the chamber, loudly admiring Chloe's decorations, saying all that she would have wished to hear. His voice was filled with enough enthusiasm to have fooled anyone else. But although Chloe was tone-deaf as far as music was concerned, she was pitch-perfect regarding voices. And in her father's voice she detected an undercurrent of something that filled her with unease.

After he had inhaled deeply of the evergreen swags adorning the windows, Sir Phineas paused in front of the picture at the far end of the room.

Chloe had woven a wreath of bright green sprigs about the oval frame of her mother's portrait.

"Bless me, child," Sir Phineas said softly. "You even remembered the rosemary."

"Aye, Papa." Chloe joined him, linking her arm through his. "Rosemary . . . for remembrance."

He said nothing but merely squeezed her hand, and for a moment the two of them stood in silence, regarding the image of Maria Waverly captured by the artist's velvet brush strokes. Mama could not have been much older than Emma now was when the sitting had been done. Clad in one of those quaint, old-fashioned gowns with the full skirts, her honey brown hair spilled over her shoulders in sausage curls, her blue eyes seemed misty, and her lips tipped in a shy smile full of secret dreamings.

Chloe had always loved the portrait and regretted that her mother had never sat for another that would have been more recent. Mama had died when Chloe had been but nine. Although the precise image of her mother had grown dim with the passing of time, memories remained of warmth and gentleness, gentle hands, gentle voice, gentle smile.

Chloe sensed that even after seven years, Papa yet mourned Mama's passing. Never in words, but in the way he sometimes gazed at the portrait, his eyes alight with tenderness, his smile melancholy.

But when Chloe gazed up at her father, she was disconcerted to see that he was not looking at the portrait but at her, and the expression on his face was one of a deeper sadness than she had ever seen before.

"Papa," she whispered. "What is it? What is wrong?"

She thought he might have answered her but for

the presence of her two sisters at the other end of the room. As it was, he merely shook his head.

"Nothing, my dear. You know what a sentimental old fool I become on Christmas Eve. It seems to be a time when memories come flooding back, often more than the heart can hold."

With that, he turned away from her, assuming the mannerisms of his usual bluff self. Striding back toward the fire, he called out, "For shame, Agnes. Close up that book. No more musty Greeks on Christmas Eve. Lucy, my dear. Open up that pianoforte and give us a song."

Chloe saw that all opportunities for confidences were at an end, especially as Mr. Henry arrived shortly thereafter. The young man had been dining at Windhaven so often of late, he seemed quite like an old friend of the family. Of course, Lucy could not resist threatening to trap the solemn clergyman under the mistletoe. He did blush so delightfully.

Emma was moved to protest as she rejoined them from the kitchens. Chloe Anne noted that Emma had removed her apron and tidied her hair. "For shame, Lucy. You should not tease poor Mr. Henry so."

"I-I do not mind, Miss Waverly," Mr. Henry stammered. "The custom of a kissing bough is pagan, and I would never permit mistletoe in the church. But in one's home, I see no harm in it."

And Chloe Anne fancied that Mr. Henry regarded her eldest sister rather hopefully, but Emma, her cheeks firing as red as his, was quick to look away.

Chloe could not say precisely that she did not enjoy the evening that followed. They had a fine dinner, and the custom of bringing in the Yule log was ever dear to her heart. She loved gathering before the fire, watching the colors leap among the flames, telling stories of ghosts and legends, days long gone by. Lucy might lament that they could not celebrate the holidays as they did in the great manors with house parties and balls, but what Chloe Anne treasured most was these quiet gatherings, her family drawn so close about her. For one night, at least, all of them were snug and secure against the world.

It would have been perfect but for her feeling that tonight somehow the world was managing to intrude. She knew not exactly how or in what form, only sensing its disturbing presence in that look of anxiety that kept creeping back into Papa's eyes.

Chloe was not sorry when the little party broke up early. Mr. Henry insisted he must get back to the vicarage to go over his sermon for the morrow, though Chloe did not doubt that he must have already rehearsed it a dozen times.

Long after she and her sisters had retired to their beds, Chloe Anne lay awake, waiting for Agnes to cease her restless tossing. The room Chloe shared with her younger sister had once been the nursery, relict of the days when they had still had a governess. Windhaven had many bedchambers, but the house was so badly in need of repairs, not many of them were habitable.

When Chloe was certain she heard the sound of Agnes's soft snoring, she slipped out of bed, draping her robe over her nightgown. Tiptoeing through the door, she crept back downstairs.

Chloe had been doing this as long as she could remember, sneaking out of bed after her sisters were asleep. Sometimes Papa sent her back to the nursery. But more often she ended up tucked on his lap while he read to her.

After she had grown too old to sit upon his knee, she had formed the custom of curling up on the rug by his feet, leaning against him. Reading had often given way to talk about matters of great importance, why fairies could no longer be found in Norfolk, what it felt like to fall in love, why a man like Napoleon would want to conquer England anyway when he could have been so much more comfortable at home by his own fireside.

When she reached the parlor, Chloe peered inside. Papa was still up, as she had known he would be. Not reading as he often did, ensconced in the wing-back chair, but simply staring into the fire, looking frighteningly old. Chloe hesitated upon the threshold, fearing that perhaps this was one night she should leave Papa alone. Whatever sorrow, whatever worry oppressed him, it might be too great, too private for him to share, even with her. As she wavered, on the verge of retreating, he looked around as though sensing her presence.

"Chloe Anne!" His voice sounded harsh, almost angry. "You should be abed, child, getting your sleep."

"Yes, I am sorry, Papa. I did not mean to disturb you."

But when she started to back away, he cried, "No, no, you are not disturbing me. 'Tis just that . . ." He raked his hand back through his graying hair with a weary sigh. "Come in, child. Come in and warm your feet by the fire. You have forgotten your slippers and will be chilled to the bone."

Chloe glanced down, for the first time noticing that her feet were bare and quite cold. Yet Papa could hardly scold. It was a failing of both of theirs, overlooking such trivialities as gloves and slippers.

Chloe approached almost shyly. She settled into a corner of the settee, tucking her feet beneath her nightgown. Papa managed to summon a smile for her, but she thought it was the saddest one she had ever seen.

"Perhaps it is just as well you have come down," he said. "I have a present for you. I meant to save it for the morrow, but now . . ." He struggled forward, heaving himself to his feet.

Chloe saw that several wrapped parcels had been deposited on the parlor table. Papa fetched the smallest one for her. She accepted it with wondering delight. Her fingers trembled with eagerness, yet she restrained herself, peeling the paper away slowly, savoring the suspense.

The object suddenly tumbled free of its wrapping, falling into her lap. Chloe saw that it was a quaint wooden carving of a very venerable-looking old gentleman attired in long robes and a flowing beard.

"I have had that tucked away for a very long time," Papa said. "So long, I had nearly forgotten it. I picked it up during my travels with the diplomatic corps in Spain."

"Who is it supposed to be, Papa? A wizard like Merlin?"

"No, my dear, it is Saint Nicholas. The Spanish believe he is the patron saint of all young, unmarried ladies."

Chloe turned the statue over in her hands, admiring the delicate and intricate carving from all angles. She was most fascinated by the heavy-lidded eyes, which looked so solemn, so wise.

"Thank you so much, Papa," she said. "Now I

shall have two guardians looking out for me, you and Saint Nicholas."

All traces of Papa's smile fled. His face resumed that expression that had so haunted her all evening. He strode abruptly to stand by the fire, his back to her.

Although a dozen fears and doubts crowded to Chloe's mind, she forced herself to remain silent, to wait patiently. At last, Papa faced her again, resting one hand heavily along the mantel, scarce noticing when he dislodged some of the holly clusters.

"Chloe Anne. There is something I must tell you. I wish it did not have to be this soon. I had wanted Christmas to be over, our revels unspoiled before I—" He broke off unhappily.

"What is it, Papa?" Chloe asked, fighting a sensation of rising alarm.

"When I was gone so long this afternoon, I did not spend all of my time at the vicarage. During part of it, I was preparing for a journey."

Her heart sank. She could not remember Papa ever being gone, not even overnight.

"What sort of journey?"

"First to London and then . . ." Sir Phineas trailed off, looking completely dispirited, but he straightened, making an effort to rally. "Actually, it is a cause for congratulations, my dear. I have managed to obtain a post again, in the diplomatic corps. What do you think of that?"

Chloe did not know what to think. She could only regard her father blankly, feeling as though her entire orderly world were suddenly being turned upside down. Of course, she had always been aware that as a young man, Papa had once had a very promising career in government service. He had achieved fame for uncovering a nefarious plot against King George. Some dissenters dissatisfied with the conduct of the American War had plotted treason, to assassinate the king. Only owing to Papa's diligence had the scheme been uncovered. The king, in his gratitude, had made Papa a knight. But that had all been so long ago. Papa had retired from civil service when he had married Mama and inherited Windhaven from his uncle.

Sir Phineas fidgeted at Chloe's lengthy silence. "I know it is sad that we have to part, but are you not pleased for me?"

Chloe forced a brittle smile to her lips. "Oh, very. Congratulations, Papa. 'Tis only that it is all so sudden."

"Not as much for me. I fear I have been writing letters for some time now to Captain William Trent. I obtained this post through his influence. You remember my mentioning Captain Trent?"

"Of course, Papa." She was not likely ever to forget Captain Trent, although she had never met the man. Windhaven was an entailed estate. Since Sir Phineas had had no sons, Captain Trent, although a very distant relative, stood to inherit Windhaven. Chloe loved her home, creaky floorboards, drafty chimneys and all. It was difficult to think that someday it would be appropriated by a total stranger. Yet she did not dwell on that grim prospect now, being pressed by a more immediate source of distress. "I am sure it was very kind of Captain Trent to help you secure a post," she said. "But, Papa, you are a knight, a landowner. Surely you have too many duties here, are far too important a man to—"

"Ah, but it is a very important position, very

grand. Only think, my dear. I am to be part of the foreign embassy in Portugal."

"Portugal!" Chloe felt herself wax pale. "Papa, there will be fighting on the Peninsula. Napoleon's army—"

"It is only Spain that has allied itself with France, my dear. Portugal is still quite safe, I assure you. I will be in no danger."

Chloe only shook her head. "Why, Papa? I don't understand why you want to do this thing."

"Well . . . er." He could not seem to meet her eyes. "You must realize that Windhaven has always been more of an encumbrance than anything. When a man reaches my age, he must give some thought to his future."

"Is it your future you are thinking of, Papa, or ours?" Chloe Anne said accusingly. "Mine and Emma's, Lucy's and Agnes's."

Sir Phineas looked sorely pressed. He flung out his hands in a helpless gesture. "Hang it all, my dear, what is so wrong with that? When a man has four daughters of marriageable age and no dowries, it is high time that he did think of their futures. A girl needs a respectable portion if she is to marry well. Indeed, marry at all."

"I don't, Papa," Chloe Anne said desperately. "I don't need a dowry or a husband. Marriage is not the only prospect. I . . . I could become a governess. I have always been fond of children. That would make one less for you to worry about and . . ."

She faltered, seeing that her argument was only causing her father to shudder, look more determined. Tears came then, falling unbidden down her cheeks. Although her father pulled forth his pocket handkerchief to check their flow, Chloe saw that there was no hope of her dissuading him from his course.

"But you could be gone so long, Papa. From all of us, from Windhaven," she whispered brokenly. "For months, perhaps years."

"Oh, tush, child. It will never be that long. And I am sure we will have soon thrashed that rascal Napoleon, making it safe to travel on the continent again. I will bring you and your sisters over. What a grand time we will have. We might even go to Paris."

"Lucy would like that." Chloe Anne sniffed.

Sir Phineas waxed eloquent with promises, wonderful visions. Although he did not quite reconcile Chloe to the imminent separation, he managed to coax a smile from her.

As he led her from the parlor, urging her to return to the warmth and comfort of her bed, he wrapped his arm about her shoulders, giving her a bracing squeeze. "After all, 'tis you I am counting upon to be the bravest, to look after your sisters in my absence."

Her? The sorriest shatterbrain in all the world? Chloe Anne gave a watery chuckle at such a ludicrous notion. "What about Emma? She is the eldest."

"So she is. I have no doubt she will see you all well fed and warmly clothed. And Lucy will be here to apprise you of the latest fashions, stay abreast of the neighborhood gossip. Agnes will be certain to keep all of your feet firmly planted on the ground, see that you remain practical. But you, my dear Chloe, will have the most important task of all."

"And what is that, Papa?"

He gave her chin a playful pinch. "You will be the Keeper of Dreams. Make sure that no one gets too sensible to indulge in a little whimsy, to keep faith when there seems little reason to do so, to believe that even the impossible can often be very possible."

Chloe thought he was teasing her but only partly so. The light in his eyes was quite tender. In any case, with utmost solemnity she gave her promise to execute his commission.

"I will, Papa," she said.

He brushed a kiss lightly upon her brow. The hall clock chiming midnight seemed to set a seal upon her pledge.

" 'Tis Christmas Day, Papa," she said. She glanced toward the windows, where little could be glimpsed but swirling whiteness set against the ebony mantle of night. "Remember the legend you told me? The one about the animals?"

"Aye. During the first hour of Christmas Day, all the beasts are said to genuflect in honor of the Christ child."

"I should like to go out some Christmas after midnight, to see if it is really true."

"Ah, but remember the rest of the legend, my dear. Anyone who catches the animals thus is said to be doomed to perish within the year."

"Then I shall wait until I am an old woman and don't care about living anymore."

"I hope you never grow to be that old, my dear."

Sir Phineas stood watching as Chloe headed up the curve of the stairs, her honey brown hair shimmering in the candlelight. So many times had this scene been played out between them, him shooing the child back to bed long after she should have been asleep. Child? Nay, no longer. Had he been so fond and foolish not to see it happening? The inches adding slowly to her height, the womanly figure starting to blossom. He seemed to have glanced away but a moment and Chloe Anne had grown up. All his daughters had.

Sir Phineas maintained his smiling posture until Chloe was swallowed by the darkness at the top of the stairs. Only then did he allow the weight of years to settle back upon him, bowing his shoulders down. He returned to the drawing room to make sure fire was banked upon the hearth, all secure.

He had always reveled in the festival of Christmas as innocently as his daughter had. It was a warm time of year, a time of memories, some bittersweet, but never any just bitter. At least not until this year.

Perhaps that was because this was the first year he had taken a long look at his life and seen what a failure it had been. He could not say what had sparked off this realization, perhaps suddenly noticing his daughters were all grown up and no provisions made for them as he ought to have done.

He had never done anything right, at least not from a worldly point of view. When he had been placed in the way of a promising government career, he had been rather hopeless, even in the role of an under secretary. Poor Chloe! Always fancying her father had been some great hero. He had uncovered the assassination plot by purest chance. It had been more his clerk's doing than his own. But the king could hardly be expected to knight some fellow of obscure parentage, whose ancestors most likely hailed from the fishmongers at Billingsgate. No, the honors had to go to Phineas, whose one virtue was that he could at least lay claim to being a gentleman. Phineas frowned into the fire at the memory. If he had been wise, he would have used his newly acquired title and his position in society to make a wealthy marriage. But at that thought, his lips had to tremble into a soft smile. How could any man who had ever glimpsed the beauty of gentle Maria Longley ever have remained wise? A vicar's daughter, she had been as poor as he, but that hadn't mattered then, that first springtime of being in love.

The heavens bless her, it still didn't matter. His marriage to Maria was the one part of his life Sir Phineas refused to count as a failure. He had inherited Windhaven shortly after the wedding, the estate already something of a ruin, the holdings burdened by his late uncle's debts. But he and Maria had retired to their new home in Norfolk to raise their brood of bright and beautiful little girls. Despite pinched purse strings, they had been happy— foolishly, deliriously happy.

That, perhaps, had been his greatest mistake. He should never have retired from government service. He should have sought out some fat sinecure of a position as other ambitious men did. But he had never been able tear himself away from his wife and daughters, from the warmth that was their home.

Even after Maria's death, he had convinced himself it was best not to leave, to seek his fortune in the city. The girls had needed him.

But on this bitter-cold Christmas Eve, he had his doubts. He could not congratulate himself that he had been a wonderful father. What good had he ever done for his daughters? He had seen that Emma was falling in love with a poverty-stricken clergyman and done nothing to stop it. Mr. Henry was such a worthy young man, and he genuinely liked the vicar. But so poor! There could scarce be a poorer living in all of England than that of St. Andrew's.

Then there was Lucy—so beautiful, so taking with her charming ways. He had indulged her too much, encouraged her small vanities until she had become discontent and restless. And Agnes—he had so delighted in her scholarly turn of mind, just what he would have wished for in a son. So he had taught her Greek and Latin, turned her into a proper little bluestocking, which would only make it more difficult for the poor child to ever acquire a husband.

But Chloe Anne—what he had done to his little Chloe was the worst of all. So lovely, so sweet, so much the image of his departed wife, it oft brought an ache to his heart. He had stuffed Chloe's head full of fantasy and legends. Even on the verge of leaving her, when he should have admonished her to be more sensible, what must he do but encourage her to keep on dreaming?

Dreams! What did they amount to anyway, Sir Phineas thought bitterly as he jabbed the poker at what remained of the glowing ashes of the fire. Only a man silly enough to try embarking on a new career at his age, a career he had never had the drive or talent for even as a youth. He could not fool himself. He would not have been able to acquire any position at all but for the intervention of his young relative.

William Trent, now there was a hero, a man who was a rising star. Before the age of thirty, the captain had become wealthy from prize ships taken, with a myriad of influential friends both in the Admiralty and the present government. Everyone predicted that Trent would be an admiral one day, his name as legend as a Nelson or a Drake.

But it profited Sir Phineas little to dwell upon

Trent's capabilities and his own inadequacies. Sighing, he put up the poker and shuffled out of the parlor. He was about to set out upon what was a useless enterprise at his age, the seeking of his fortune; but he had to try. The impossible could be possible. He needed to believe that more than he had ever needed to before.

Ah, but leaving his little girls, that was going to be the hardest part. He paused by the window in the vast silent front hall to utter a silent prayer, commending his daughters to the care of more skilled hands than his own inept ones.

When he had finished, a sense of peace settled over him as tranquil as the falling snow. By nature, Sir Phineas was a man framed for optimism. Something was bound to come right. Good fortune was just around the bend, and all he had to do was put himself in its way.

With the suppression of his nagging doubts, he began to feel the need for sleep, but it was a more mellow feeling of exhaustion. Yet he had one last task to perform before going to bed.

They had only one groom left at Windhaven these days, and Dan was rather young, not always to be relied upon. Sir Phineas had ridden his sorrel mare rather hard today. He would just check to be certain that the animal had been properly rubbed down and was secure for the night.

Swirling his cape about his shoulders, Sir Phineas let himself out the kitchen door, which was the closest route to the stable yard. It was snowing hard now, the wind whipping the blinding whiteness into his face, threatening to extinguish the lantern he carried.

His head tucked down, he made his way forward by dint of following the low-lying hedge that surrounded the garden. The tops of his ears were freezing, but his hearing remained keen enough to catch a faint sound above the whistle of the wind.

A lowing sound.

Sir Phineas paused in astonishment until he realized that the foolish dairy cow they kept must have somehow gotten out of her shed again and wandered into the garden.

Raising one hand to shield his eyes, he peered over the hedge and saw that he was right. He could just make out a bulky brown form, but . . .

Sir Phineas's heart did a sudden leap. The animal appeared to have fallen to its knees just as if it were paying homage. No! Phineas placed his numbed fingers against his eyes and rubbed. What he had been about to think was absurd. He had been regaling Chloe with far too many old legends. He was starting to believe them himself.

Struggling past the hedge, he sought to drive the cow back into her shed. When he reached her side, she was standing upright. Either the beast had floundered in the white drifts, then managed to right herself, or the whole vision had been merely a trick of the blinding snow.

As he closed the cow back up in her stall, he chuckled to himself, imagining Chloe's reaction when he entertained her with his foolish fancy in the morning.

But in the bustle of Christmas and the preparations for his imminent departure, the incident passed from Sir Phineas's mind, and he entirely forgot to mention it.

Chapter 1

December, 1807

The HMS *Gloriana* rocked against her moorings in Plymouth Harbor. Pale morning sunlight streamed through the stern windows into the spacious cabin Captain William Trent shared with a twelve-pound cannon. The chamber contained none of the luxuries most wealthy officers deemed necessary. Besides the cannon, the furnishings consisted of no more than a cot dangling from the deck beam, a sea chest, a chair, and the desk bolted to the wall.

Seated hunched over the desk, Captain Trent dipped his quill into the inkwell, trying to finish his report to the Admiralty and his request for the material necessary to refit his ship for sea duty. Shadows from the hanging lantern played across his crop of thick, dark hair and aristocratic features set into lines even more formidable than usual. He was of medium height, and his lean, hard body was as solid-iron as the ship's anchor, more suited for action than desk work. Composing reports was not among Trent's more favored activities, and he already felt a cramp in his hand.

Even as he scratched his quill across the page, Trent gritted his teeth, knowing that it was an exercise in futility. No matter how eloquent his appeal, he would be lucky to get even half of the ordnance supplies, provisions, and men that he asked for.

When his pen spluttered ink across the page, Trent swore softly, his concentration further hampered by the presence of his steward in the cabin. The burly seaman was cheerily going about the task of transferring some of Trent's things from the sea chest to a smaller trunk in preparation for a fortnight's shore leave.

While he worked, Mr. Samuel Doughty persisted in whistling some tuneless ditty, employing the gap between his front teeth to great advantage. After enduring this for a few moments, Trent flung down his pen and shifted around.

"Mr. Doughty!" he snapped.

"Cap'n?" The steward's head popped up from behind the sea chest, his bristling side-whiskers giving him the appearance of a startled walrus.

Trent merely frowned, fixing the steward with his steely gaze. His eyes were the hue of the sea at its coldest, a wintery gray. It took Doughty a moment of soul-searching to realize the nature of his offense.

"Oh! The whistling again. Sorry, Cap'n, I do try hard to remember. That is, aye, aye, Cap'n. I won't nary do it again."

When Trent arched his brow, Doughty took another pause for reflection before brightening. "That is, I won't be doing it again, *sir*," he said with a gap-toothed grin.

"Thank you, Mr. Doughty." Trent turned back to his desk in time to hide a smile. Doughty's grin was as infectious as the man was incorrigible. Over a year under Trent's command had been insufficient to teach the rogue the proper way to address his captain.

A captured smuggler, Doughty had chosen the king's service over the king's noose. He had arrived on Trent's ship in irons, pale, emaciated, but full of so much impudence, no amount of time beneath the lash could have cured him of it.

Trent had tried patience instead, striking off the man's chains, treating him like a human being again. And Trent's forbearance had been rewarded. Doughty proved the best steward he had ever had, as handy at darning a uniform as any housewife, able to miraculously manage hot meals for his captain even during the worst of storms. Now if only Trent could break the fellow of his infernal habit of whistling . . .

For the moment, at least, silence was restored. Trent turned back to his writing, but he had not progressed much further when Doughty began clearing his throat with a series of loud harrumphs, trying to gain Trent's attention.

"What is it now, Mr. Doughty?" He put down his quill.

"Beggin' yer pardon, Cap'n. Don't mean to be disturbin' ye again, sir. But I was wishful to know: Be this the uniform ye want me to be packin' for yer weddin' day?"

Trent cast a cursory glance over the garment Doughty held aloft, Trent's best blue jacket, gold epaulets glittering on the shoulders, buttons gleaming down the front.

"No, Mr. Doughty. I won't be wearing any uniform. Pack my dark gray frock coat."

Doughty's look of dismay was almost comical. "Fer yer weddin', Cap'n?"

"Yes." Trent leveled him a fierce stare. "I take it that does not meet with your approval?"

"No, sir! Er ... that is, I suppose it be not my place to say anything."

"That seldom prevents you from saying it. And what is wrong with my gray coat, pray?"

Doughty hemmed and hawed. " 'Tis just when a gent stands up with a lady, 'specially for the purposes of matrimony, well, he needs to spread his feathers a bit, kind'a like the way a peacock does for his peahen."

Trent's lips twitched with amusement, but he replied gravely enough, "I fear my peahen is too sensible to be impressed by my naval plumage."

"Nay, don't you believe it, sir. All ladies be set aflutter by a man in uniform. I don't fancy Miss Emma Waverly could be that much different from the lot o' females."

"I don't recall ever mentioning the lady's name, Mr. Doughty. Have you been reading my correspondence?"

"No, sir!" Doughty's eyes widened, the very picture of wounded innocence. " 'Tis just when mail is left lying about, it's hard sometimes not to notice a name, and I always can tell a lady's handwritin'. I be somethin' of an expert on the ladies, Cap'n."

"So you have informed me upon several occasions, Mr. Doughty."

The steward puffed out his chest. "Yes, sir, I came close to tying the knot meself several times, but the fathers of the young ladies were never quite fast enough to catch up with me. That 'minds me of another reason to wear yer uniform, sir. It might go a long way to impress and soften yer future papa-in-law."

"That is not something I need to worry about.

Miss Waverly's father is—" Trent broke off, suddenly no longer finding anything amusing about the conversation.

"Carry on, Mr. Doughty," he said sharply. "I should like to see my packing finished sometime this year."

"Ay, aye, Cap'n." The big man looked puzzled by his captain's sudden reversion to coldness. But Trent was not about to offer any further explanation.

Bending over the desk once more, he retrieved his quill, but the pen remained idle between his fingers, the words on the report before him no more than a meaningless jumble of ink strokes. Doughty's idle chatter had triggered off unfortunate reflections, memories that Trent found less than pleasant.

Try to impress Miss Waverly's father, his future papa-in-law, Doughty had counseled him. Would to God he had such a concern, Trent thought bitterly. But one didn't need to worry about currying the good opinion of a man encased in a shroud, full fathoms deep off the coast of Portugal.

Trent's frown deepened, and the sounds of the ship creaking and the thud of footsteps above him on the *Gloriana*'s quarterdeck slowly faded. Relentlessly, Trent's memories carried him back to the time nearly two years ago when he had captained another vessel, the frigate *Corolla*.

Trent had but to close his eyes and he could almost feel the *Corolla*'s deck trembling beneath him, hear the roar of the cannon fire from the Spanish man-of-war that brought the *Corolla*'s masthead crashing down.

Outmanned and outgunned, Trent had sought desperately to save his ship. His hand clasped his blood-soaked shoulder, where a musket ball had lodged. Acrid smoke stinging his eyes, he had barked out a series of sharp commands, trying to restore order. The deck around him had erupted into a chaos of tangled rigging and splintered wood, screams of wounded and dying men. To add to the disaster, one of the *Corolla*'s cannons had broken free and now careened across the desk, a ton and a half of lethal, crushing iron.

It was in the midst of this hell that Trent had glimpsed Sir Phineas Waverly struggling to maintain his balance on a deck slickened with blood, striving to reach the side of a fallen cabin boy.

Battling his own fatigue and pain as well as the enemy ship, Trent had been enraged to see the old man flout his orders to remain in the hold with the other diplomats.

"Sir Phineas!" Trent had bellowed. "Get below."

But as the cabin boy lolled back lifelessly, the elderly knight straightened and actually seemed to be heading toward Trent.

"Get back!" Trent called, his shout less in anger than in warning this time. But even his quarterdeck roar could not rise above the thunder of another broadside from the Spanish ship. Trent was never sure if the old man had even heard him. . . .

A brisk knocking at his door brought Trent forcibly back from the beleaguered *Corolla*, back to the present and the calm of the *Gloriana*'s cabin. Trent shook off his memories, calling out a command to enter.

The sentry who stood posted outside came in to announce, "Begging your pardon, sir, but there is a Mr. Charles Lathrop requesting permission to come on board."

"Granted," Trent said. "Have Mr. Lathrop escorted to my cabin at once."

With a smart salute, the sentry exited to pass on the order. Trent gestured to his steward, who was just folding several of Trent's cravats into the trunk.

"You can finish the packing later, Mr. Doughty, after I have done meeting with Mr. Lathrop. Right now, I want you to go topside and inform Lieutenant Bennington that I want a word with him before I am piped ashore."

"Aye, aye, Cap'n." Doughty was quick to agree but not so quick to act. He was still shuffling about the cabin when the door was opened by the sentry, returning to usher in the Honorable Charles Lathrop.

Trent allowed himself few luxuries, and that included friends. But despite himself, he had developed a close acquaintanceship with Charles Lathrop, whom Trent had known from the days of his boyhood.

As he rose to his feet, Trent felt a stirring of pleasure at the sight of the friend he had not seen for nigh on a year. A pleasant-featured man, Lathrop wore a caped coat with a single modest cape fashioned after the manner of a country gentleman.

Sweeping off his high-crowned beaver hat, he had to stoop slightly when entering the cabin to avoid banging his head of wavy brown hair against the deck beam. Spying Trent, Lathrop grinned, coming smartly to attention with a mock salute.

"Permission to come on board, sir."

"You already have it, Lathrop. Or else my watch would have long since peppered your wherry with shot." Smiling, Trent stepped forward, extending his hand.

Lathrop was the sort of exuberant fellow who

would have embraced him, but he knew Trent well enough not to attempt such a thing. Instead, Lathrop contented himself with a hearty handclasp.

His eyes twinkled. "By God, you are looking fit, you old pirate. As bronzed and weather-beaten as any Jack-Tar. You make me feel pale as a sheet by comparison."

"You are," Trent said equably.

Lathrop's gaze skated round the cabin, coming to rest on the steward. "And here is your faithful Mr. Doughty. What, Mr. Doughty! Still here? You have managed to survive another voyage under this tyrant? I thought you would have jumped ship long 'ere now."

"No, sir." Mr. Doughty looked pleased that Lathrop had remembered him. And yet . . . Was it just Trent's imagination, or had Doughty given a guilty start at Lathrop's jest? Trent hoped it was only his fancy. It would be disturbing to think that Doughty contemplated such mischief. Desertion was a far more serious crime than smuggling.

But Doughty appeared easy enough, his everready grin widening his lips. "I had to hang about, Mr. Lathrop. I wouldn't miss the captain's wedding for next month's tot o' rum."

"Wedding?" Lathrop echoed, looking astounded as well he might. Trent had informed few people of his forthcoming nuptials.

"That will do, Mr. Doughty," he said testily.

Doughty ambled toward the door and exited with a salute, that is, as close as the rogue ever came to executing a proper one. When the door closed behind him, Trent was left to face Lathrop's questioning gaze.

Trent avoided it for a moment by inviting Lathrop to have a seat. He pulled a face at the hard, straight-backed chair but lowered himself into it, tossing his hat upon the desk.

"You don't waste much of your prize money on the amenities, do you, Trent? Like a more comfortable chair."

"It would only mean that much more rubbish to be cleared away for action." Trent took up a position near the cannon, leaning against the great iron barrel. "And how are your mother and sisters, Charles? Well, I trust?"

"Oh, quite well." Lathrop made an impatient gesture. He was not about to be put off by such pleasantries. "Never mind about my family. What was that nonsense Doughty was sprouting about weddings?"

"It was not nonsense, but quite true. Though this is scarce the blunt manner in which I meant to announce the fact, I fear I must call upon you, Charles, to offer me felicitations. I am about to be married."

"The devil, you say!" Lathrop let out a long, low whistle of amazement. "I knew Lady Caroline had set her cap at you, but I can see I never gave the woman enough credit by half. To have snared you when you are so seldom off the deck of a ship—"

"Do not become too lost in your admiration of Caroline. It is not she who has brought me to the altar, but another lady."

"Dear me. I have heard you sailors have a girl in every port. So who is this fortunate damsel? Am I to be privileged to know her name?"

"Certainly. I am betrothed to Miss Emma Waverly."

Lathrop's face fell, his teasing manner swiftly abandoned. "Waverly! You . . . you don't mean the daughter of that old man who perished aboard your ship that time, the one who . . . who—"

"Yes, precisely. Sir Phineas Waverly."

When Lathrop lapsed into a troubled silence, Trent stirred restively. "You need not look as though my betrothal were something unnatural or even uncommon, Charles. After all, Sir Phineas was a distant relative of sorts. When he died, I not only inherited his estate but also the guardianship of his four daughters, with the exception of Miss Emma, who is already of age."

Lathrop shook his head as though he could still not take it in. "But, Trent, I thought . . . That is, I mean, have you ever even met this girl?"

"No. Unfortunately, my duties have prevented me from ever visiting Windhaven. But I have had frequent correspondence with Miss Waverly."

"Indeed, you receive mail so often when you are on board ship. How often have you written each other? Once? Twice?"

"Enough," Trent said evasively. "With your romantic nature, Charles, I thought you would find the tale of my courtship quite pleasing."

Lathrop rose to his feet and paced off a few steps, as much as the cabin would let him. His usually smooth brow was knit with worry. "If I saw any romance in this, mayhap I would, but what I fear I see is guilt."

"That's ridiculous."

"Is it?" Lathrop gave him a long, searching stare which Trent found he could not meet. "My God, Trent," he went on. "You cannot continue to hold yourself responsible for the death of that old man."

"Can't I? He would never have been aboard that ship but for me."

"Aye, you tried to do him a kindness, going to a great deal of effort, getting him that post in the diplomatic corps."

"Kindness!" Trent snorted. It had been a very careless sort of kindness. When Sir Phineas had first approached him for his aid, Trent had been in excellent humor, having newly acquired the stripes that marked him as a captain with seniority. In the flush of those spirits, he had glibly promised Sir Phineas anything. And, indeed, getting the old man his post had proved no hardship. Just the whisper in the right ear of an influential acquaintance in the government . . .

"You never expected Sir Phineas to be sent to Portugal," Lathrop continued to argue. "Any more than you thought to convey him on your ship. Any more than you expected to run afoul of that Spanish man-of-war. And you did order the old man to stay below."

"Aye," Trent said wearily, knowing it was useless to argue with Lathrop, useless to expect anyone raised outside the tradition of the navy to understand the one simple fact. The captain was always ultimately responsible for what happened aboard his ship, for the lives of every man, be he crew or passenger.

"Wasn't it wonderfully convenient?" Trent sneered with some bitterness. "To have Sir Phineas die aboard my ship, me being his heir."

"Damnation!" Lathrop flushed a bright red. "You know, if anyone else dared imply such a thing, I'd call them out. As if you ever coveted that old man's ramshackle estate! I daresay it will take half your own fortune to bring it to any kind of order."

"I daresay it would, if I meant to try. But I am more concerned with the fate of Sir Phineas's orphaned daughters."

"So much so that you intend to sacrifice yourself on the altar of matrimony."

"Don't be so dramatic, Charles, and do check your agitation before you forget yourself and crack your head on one of the deck beams." Trent added in almost placating tones, "It's no good your remonstrating with me, Charles. My course is set. I have proposed to Miss Waverly, and she has accepted me. We will be wed at Windhaven during the upcoming Christmas holidays."

Lathrop shot him a look seething with frustration, but he sank back into the chair, flinging out his hands in resignation.

"I suppose it only remains for me to wish you joy, then. Lord, won't Lady Caroline look blue when she hears of this."

"Perhaps, but not for very long, I trust. There was never any deep attachment between us."

"Only because you would not permit it."

"No, I wouldn't," Trent said. "That is one of the important lessons I learned from my grandfather, the admiral. He taught me that a captain has no business forming close attachments, neither with his crew nor with those he leaves behind on shore. You know well what my life is like, Charles. A month at home, then years at sea. I have scarce been off the deck of a ship since I was nine, one of the privileges of being an admiral's grandson."

"Oh, aye, a rare privilege that," Lathrop interrupted dryly.

Trent ignored him. "It would be a cruelty for me to inspire a great love in any lady only to leave her pining for months on end. Cruel to us both. Far better to wed without passion. I am sure Miss Waverly and I will grow to be fond enough of each other without being clinging. Her letters mark her to be a most sensible young woman."

"I hope she is at least pretty. Have you ever seen a portrait of her?"

"No, but Sir Phineas always used to speak of her as being quite lovely."

"Fathers are ridiculously partial that way. My own sire used to think my sisters beauties, and you know quite well that both Lydia and Bess have more freckles than there are shells in the sea. For all you know, Miss Waverly may be the the image of her papa."

Perhaps she would be, but that meant little to Trent. It often disturbed him that Sir Phineas's image had faded so from his memory. He recollected little of the elderly knight except that he had had a pair of very kindly eyes.

"Sir Phineas was an exceedingly strange old man," Trent mused aloud. "I must confess, at times I found him an infernal nuisance when he was on board. He had a habit of seeking me out to talk, even when I was taking my solitary stroll on the quarterdeck. Though God knows what he spoke of. I can scarce remember." He gave a reluctant laugh. "Sometimes I had the feeling he harbored the peculiar notion that I was lonely."

"Peculiar indeed," Lathrop murmured, casting Trent an oddly penetrating stare.

Trent gave himself a little shake as though to rid himself of the reminiscing mood he seemed to have fallen into of late. "I didn't mean to wax so long-winded," he said apologetically. "I ought to be explaining why I sent for you, dragged you all the way down here to Plymouth."

"I should thing this leveler about your upcoming marriage reason enough."

"Oh, I could have conveyed that in a letter. I fear there is something more." Trent felt a rare surge of emotion and spoke more gruffly to conceal it. "I should deem it a great favor if you would travel up to Windhaven to stand up with me at my wedding."

"I should have deemed it a great insult if you hadn't asked me." Lathrop leapt up impulsively, and Trent feared he would not escape an embrace this time. But Lathrop expressed the force of his feelings with a cuff to Trent's shoulder.

"You great dolt! Of course I shall come. And you must have known that. Why else would you have 'dragged me all the way to Plymouth,' as you put it?"

"I suppose I was rather sure of your answer. I fear I presume too much upon your good nature."

"No," Lathrop said earnestly. "You presume upon the basis of our friendship, as well you should."

"Yes, well ... ahem." Trent gave an embarrassed cough and edged a few paces away from him. "Good. That's all settled, then, though I do feel a little guilty for taking you away from your own family at Christmastime."

"That is no hardship, believe me. My mother has invited a parcel of her tonnish friends down from London and is busy planning a ball, a masquerade, and all manner of other horrors. You know how I despise all that fashionable nonsense. You have sailed to my rescue, Captain Trent. If only you could be married every Christmas."

"Once, I trust, will suffice. I have been given a leave of absence by the Admiralty. We have only to agree on our traveling arrangements. By post, I thought. Could you possibly be ready to set out today?"

"Within the hour." Lathrop retrieved his hat and gave it a playful toss, catching it by the brim. "How long has the Admiralty given you? One month? Two?"

"A fortnight only."

"Well! I call that a rather shabby allotment for a man's wedding and bride trip."

"There will be no bride trip. The Admiralty is not romantic, Charles. And even though things have not been quite so heated since Trafalgar, there is still a war going on."

"So there is." Lathrop sobered but only for a moment. "But not in Norfolk. There we shall cry down with the fierce god Mars. It shall be Venus to whom we pay our court. You did say Waverly had four daughters?" Lathrop preened a little, straightening his cravat. "Perhaps I shall set up an agreeable flirtation with one of the younger ones."

Trent bit back a smile. Like Mr. Doughty, Lathrop fancied himself quite a devil with the ladies. The truth was that Lathrop possessed far too sweet a disposition to ever cut a dash as a rakehell.

All the same, Trent humored him, growling, "You had best control your libertine propensities, Charles, and recollect that those three young ladies are my wards. I might be forced to call you out."

"I tremble with fear, *mon capitaine*," Charles mocked. After a little more jesting in this vein, the time and place of their departure was fixed upon, and Charles took his leave to see to his own packing.

Trent caught himself still smiling long after Lathrop had left him. He wondered, not for the first time, how such a somber fellow as himself had retained a friendship with a man as jovial as Charles. Perhaps because contrary to Admiral Sefton's teachings, one did not lightly shake off the attachments of one's youth.

Trent had never had brother or sister, his mother dying in the birthing of him. His scholarly father had seemed but a gentle shadow passing through his life. Trent's whole world had been dominated by the gruff old man who had been his grandfather. Rear Admiral John Sefton had taken Trent aboard his own flagship and made him a midshipman at the tender age of nine. Though Trent had never doubted his fierce grandfather's love for him, the admiral had shown Trent no quarter, done nothing to spare him the rigors of life at sea.

Only once had the admiral ever exerted his influence on Trent's behalf. That was when the eleven-year-old Trent had been wounded in action, a flying splinter the size of a knife driven through his thigh.

The admiral had had Trent removed from shipboard and the inept ship surgeon's care. He had sent his grandson to convalesce at the home of old family acquaintances, the Lathrops. It was during those three months that a bond had been forged between Trent and Charles Lathrop, a friendship that had endured against all the changes of maturing, the necessarily long separations. Rather than being at school in the manner of most boys his age and station, eight-year-old Charles had been kept at home with a tutor because his mama had feared for his "delicate constitution."

How anyone could have fancied Charles delicate, observing the mad way he rode his horse at fences, Trent had not known or cared. He had been only too glad of Charles's company.

That had been a glorious summer of hunting for birds' nests, swimming in the pond, playing at cricket, simply being a boy instead of Mr. Midshipman Trent of His Majesty's flagship *Diana*.

Trent had never forgotten those halcyon days.

They remained among his fondest memories. He was still reflecting upon them when Mr. Doughty returned to the cabin.

Trent snapped to at once, ashamed to be caught woolgathering. While Doughty finished up the packing, Trent made haste to finish his report.

He was just inking in his name with his usual precision when Doughty closed up the trunk and announced, "There now. That's all square, Cap'n."

"Very good, Mr. Doughty. Convey the trunk topside."

"Aye, aye, sir. And I just want to be thanking you, sir, fer taking me with you. I haven't been off this ship since they brought me from the excises. I've never seen Norfolk, but I hear tell they have a fine coastline. Plenty of prime coves for smuggling."

When Trent glanced up sharply, Doughty flashed a bright smile.

"Only jesting, sir."

"I sincerely hope so, Mr. Doughty. Just as I hope you will contain some of your enthusiasm and recollect that at the end of two weeks, we will be back here aboard ship. *Both of us.*"

"Indeed. O'course, sir," Doughty responded glibly.

Trent frowned, experiencing again that stirring of uneasiness, wondering if he was making a mistake trusting the roguish steward. He might have been wrong to request the use of Doughty's services away from the ship. Taking him inland might only set the most dreadful temptation in the man's way.

But Trent was swiftly distracted from these troubling thoughts. Moving to close the sea chest, Doughty let out a loud howl, followed by a string of curses.

"What the devil is amiss now, Mr. Doughty?" Trent demanded. "Did you smash your thumb?"

The steward's face was puckered into an expression of dismay that appeared ludicrously childlike on such a brawny fellow.

"No, Cap'n, beggin' yer pardon, sir, but 'tis pure calamity, that's what it is. Look what happened during that last squall that bumped your sea chest about."

Doughty's hand trembled a little as he delved into the chest and drew forth what looked like no more than a handful of crumbled stone. When it finally occurred to Trent what had broken, he shrugged.

"It was only the figurine that Greek sea captain insisted upon giving me," Trent said. "Just a casting of Saint somebody or other."

"Saint Nicholas, Cap'n," Doughty said reproachfully. "Saint Nicholas, the protector of all sailors. Oh, woe betide! This be an ill omen, sir. Best postpone all your plans, the shore leave and the wedding!"

"Don't be ridiculous."

Doughty was appallingly superstitious, like most seamen, and Trent had little patience with it. He ordered the steward to dispose of the broken pieces, then see to removing his baggage to the quarterdeck.

Although Doughty moved to obey, he shook his head darkly. Even as he hoisted the trunk to his shoulder and left the cabin, Trent could still hear him muttering lamentations beneath his breath, the dire prediction that he never expected to live to see his captain exchange vows with Miss Emma Waverly.

Partly amused, partly exasperated, Trent moved to close up the sea chest himself when Doughty had gone. As he lowered the lid, he noticed the steward had missed one of the chunks of statue.

Reaching down, Trent drew forth the saint's decapitated head. The stone eyes did seem to regard him with a cold blankness that was a little macabre. But as Trent was not in the least superstitious, he marched to the stern and forced open one of the windows. Without further thought, he cast the head of Saint Nicholas into the foam-capped depths of the Channel.

Chapter 2

The time had come to put away all black bands, ribbons, and other signs of mourning. If only memories were as easily packed away, Chloe Anne thought with a sigh. Slipping the mourning ring from her finger, she laid it to rest in the top drawer of her dresser with the other treasured reminders of her father, the fob and watch he had worn as a young man, the small wooden carving of Saint Nicholas, Sir Phineas's final letter to her.

A year and a half had passed since the notice had come from Captain Trent bearing the dreadful tidings. The first torrents of her grief had eased to become a gentle rain. She could even derive some solace at the thought that at least now Papa must be reunited with her mother. She did not doubt that from some distant heaven both her parents kept watch over their four daughters.

Chloe almost envied them, for there was little of heaven apparent this day in Norfolk. The sky beyond the nursery room's latticed windows was a most dismal winter gray. Tension seemed to crackle in the air as sharply as the green logs on the fire.

At least Chloe felt the tension, though she was not sure either Lucy or Agnes did. This waiting, waiting, waiting for the arrival of Captain William Trent was somehow like anticipating the onslaught of a storm. Captain Trent—her guardian. It became a formidable word when applied to a stranger. To feel oneself at the complete disposal of a gentleman one didn't even know—it was more than a little frightening.

Chloe wondered how Agnes could look so unconcerned. The girl sprawled on her stomach before the hearth, propped up by her elbows as she perused a book. Agnes seemed to be developing a squint, doubtlessly from eyestrain. At the moment, she was engrossed in Euclid's *Elements*, a treatise on geometry. The title alone was enough to give Chloe a headache.

Wistfully, she turned her gaze to Lucy instead, but her older sister did not seem to be thinking of anything more than the stitches she was setting into one of Chloe's old gowns. Perched on the edge of the four-poster bed, Lucy frowned as she struggled with the needle. Snapping the thread, she suppressed a vexed exclamation as she pricked her finger. She held up one smooth, white hand, carefully examining it for any sign of a scratch.

"There, Chloe Anne," she said crossly, fairly tossing the gown at Chloe. "That is the best I can do."

Chloe caught up the folds of blue wool gratefully. She had been standing in her shift the entire time while Lucy stitched. A draft whistled through the nursery windows that not even the blazing fire could offset. Chloe's arms prickled with gooseflesh.

Hurriedly, she wriggled into the gown while Lucy came to lace up the back. Chloe surveyed herself critically in the long pier glass. The image reflected back displayed to her a spritely young woman with flowing honey brown hair. Somehow she had always expected to be much taller when she reached the age of eighteen. She supposed that she might as well give over wishing for any more inches.

With the gown smoothed into place, Chloe saw that Lucy had managed quite well with the hem. There really had been no need to let it down by much. However, the bodice was still uncomfortably snug.

Chloe stood sidewise, ruefully surveying the pert outline of her curves. "And to think I could not wait until I had acquired a bosom," she murmured. "It has turned out to be a great nuisance."

"It wouldn't be if your gowns fit you properly," Lucy grumbled. "You might spend some of your allowance to have more fashionable ones made."

Lucy certainly had done so. She was smartly attired in a high-waisted yellow gown, set off by a spencer of apple green taffeta. With her golden blond beauty and willowy figure, the effect was quite charming.

Each of them was now possessed of a generous quarterly allowance, owing to the pension and death benefits Papa had received from the government. Chloe would sooner have been a pauper condemned to a workhouse if only that would have meant the return of her father.

Lucy continued to regard Chloe's old gown with an expression of distaste. "You might at least have ordered yourself one new frock for Captain Trent's visit, Chloe Anne. I cannot imagine what you have been wasting all your money upon."

"I can," Agnes chimed in, without looking up from her book. She still possessed the remarkable ability to read and follow a conversation at the same time. "Chloe opens her purse to every beggar who walks down the lane, to say nothing of slipping money to old Mr. Kirk to do some carpentry work on the west wing of the house."

Chloe scowled at Agnes, tempted, not for the first time, to take one of Agnes's heavy tomes and thunk her over the head with it. Chloe waxed rather sheepish as Lucy fixed scolding eyes upon her.

"Oh, Chloe, you know full well Windhaven belongs to Captain Trent now, even if he has been good enough to let us stay on here. He has hired his own bailiff to look after things, and you shouldn't interfere."

"Mr. Martin?" Chloe pronounced the spindly bailiff's name with loathing. "He's a clutch-fisted old fool. All he will ever do is thrust his pointed nose in the air and declare that he has no authority to waste the captain's money on needless repairs. Meanwhile, Windhaven is going to rack and ruin."

"Windhaven always was a ruin," Agnes said with gloomy satisfaction.

"Then the captain needs must do something to save it."

"No, he doesn't," Agnes replied. "He may not choose to fling his fortune away on Windhaven. Parts of the house are already quite hopeless."

Chloe opened her mouth to hotly refute her sister's comment, but an uneasy memory stayed her tongue. Mr. Kirk had said pretty much the same thing when Chloe had gone through the old west wing with him.

"See those doors, Miss Chloe? They don't hang right, and those stairs are starting to list. Like as not, the foundation has gone bad. Perhaps the house was not built proper to begin with."

"It has managed to remain standing for two hundred years, Mr. Kirk," Chloe had informed him proudly.

"Well, I daresay it will never hold up for another two hundred. I wouldn't even give it twenty. By far the cheapest course would be to knock it all down and start over again."

Knock down Windhaven? The old carpenter's suggestion still appalled Chloe Anne. What! Sweep away over two centuries of grace and charm and history? She would never permit it except . . . Chloe constantly had to stop and keep reminding herself that Windhaven was no longer in truth her home. It belonged to this captain now. But surely he must realize the value of the estate.

"And why else would Captain Trent be coming here?" Chloe caught herself insisting aloud. "Except to see about restoring Windhaven."

Lucy gave an impatient sniff. "To arrange something about our futures, I hope, instead of worrying about a creaky old house. I do not intend to spend the rest of my life buried at Windhaven. It was very tiresome and arbitrary of Captain Trent to advise Emma that we should all remain quietly here in Norfolk until he gets around to deciding what to do with us. Not even permitting me to visit my own cousins in London! Why, it's positively barbaric."

Although Chloe was not exactly in charity with the captain herself, she felt obliged to be fair. "I suppose it was the most sensible course for the captain to follow. He would be held accountable if any harm came to us, traveling about. I daresay he doesn't want to make any hasty decisions until he becomes better acquainted with us."

"Well, he has had plenty of opportunity to do that. He could have called upon us during the past year."

"He is a naval captain, Lucy," Agnes said, her voice laced with sarcasm. "There is the little matter of trying to stop Napoleon's plans to launch an invasion fleet."

"I don't see any need for Captain Trent to feel obliged to do it single-handedly. There are plenty of other men in the navy, you know." Lucy strutted before the mirror, pausing to pinch some color into her cheeks—an unnecessary gesture, as her face was already flushed with indignation. "Captain Trent or no Captain Trent, I don't intend to miss the London Season this year."

"Much good it will do you." Agnes smirked as she turned another page. "The allowance you have been drawing scarce constitutes a fortune."

Lucy tossed her golden curls. "I don't care. Other women have made successful matches with nothing more than beauty to recommend them. Why shouldn't I?" A hardness crept into Lucy's eyes. Chloe had seen that look come over her sister too often of late, and she did not like it. In some strange way, it diminished Lucy's beauty.

"By this time next year," Lucy declared, "I am going to be wed to a lord, at the very least, and be hideously, fabulously wealthy."

"And very much in love too, I hope," Chloe added anxiously.

Lucy gave her a look of lofty disdain. "Do strive for a little maturity, Chloe Anne. Love has nothing to do with marriage."

"It did for Mama and Papa."

Lucy appeared momentarily taken aback by this quiet reminder, but she was quick to rally. "Oh, but that was a long time ago. Things were very different then. These are modern times, Chloe. At present, all I want to do is make a good impression on this dreary captain, convince him that he need only point me toward London and wash his hands of me."

So saying, Lucy turned back to the mirror. Although her toilette was already quite perfect, she spent the next several minutes primping, fussing with the folds of her skirt, until Chloe began to feel self-conscious and stole a second peek at her own appearance.

Although she hated to admit it, she was both nervous and excited at the prospect of meeting this unknown naval officer. More than anything, she longed to ply Captain Trent with questions about her father's last hours. His report had seemed so curt, so unsatisfactory.

The hardest thing about losing Papa had been the suddenness with which he seemed to disappear from their lives. They had not even been able to mourn over him, lay him to rest in the family crypt. Papa had simply vanished, consigned to the depths of the cold, cruel sea.

There was so much Chloe Anne felt she still needed to know about Sir Phineas's last days. And yet she wondered if she would ever have the courage to make inquiries of this captain, who was a complete stranger.

"What do you suppose he is like, this Captain Trent?" Chloe Anne asked her sisters.

Lucy stopped primping long enough to consider this question. "I don't know. I have never really thought about it. One of those stiff-necked military types, I suppose."

"I daresay he is like most sea captains," Agnes piped up. "Coarse, with a booming voice, bandy legs, and a flaming red nose because he drinks too much rum."

"Pooh," Lucy said. "How would you know? How many sea captains have you ever met?"

But Lucy looked a little daunted all the same. Agnes was so well read. She had a way of knowing about these things. As for Chloe, she found Agnes's description positively alarming. But before either she or Lucy could press Agnes for the source of her information, they were interrupted by a knock on the bedchamber door.

The maid, Polly, thrust her head inside long enough to announce, "If you please, young ladies, Miss Emma is wishful of having a word with you belowstairs in the drawing room."

When Polly ducked out, the three sisters exchanged uneasy glances. They were not usually so formal in their household. The last time they had all been thus summoned it was to find Emma, red-eyed, the letter from Captain Trent clasped in her hand as she steeled herself to inform them about Papa.

"Now what's amiss?" Agnes slapped her book closed and sat up. But her sharp tone did a poor job of concealing her anxiety.

"Do you think that anything has happened to Great Aunt Martha?" Lucy asked.

"Oh, no, I am sure it is nothing terrible," Chloe Anne said, although she was sure of no such thing. But she sought to reassure her younger sister, taking Agnes's cold hand within her own. For once, Agnes let her.

The three of them crept downstairs to the drawing room, huddling upon the threshold to peer inside. Emma was perched primly in Papa's wingback chair, her hands folded in her lap. She looked composed, not at all as though she had been weeping, but Emma was good at concealing such things.

Since she had turned twenty-two, she had adopted a habit of tucking her soft brown hair beneath a lace cap. Emma only wore it loose, Chloe had noticed, on those days the Reverend Mr. Henry came to tea. This afternoon Emma's cap was fixed firmly in place.

She summoned a smile at the sight of her sisters. "Come in, my dears. Do not look so alarmed. It is not anything so very dreadful I have to tell you, I promise you."

Her words reassured Lucy and Agnes, but not Chloe. Emma's eyes appeared serene, but there was great unhappiness present all the same. Chloe heard it in her voice.

Lucy flounced onto the settee, sitting down in a swirl of taffeta. "Then, Emma, I do wish you would not make such a piece of work about it. You frightened us half to death with that summons."

"I am sorry. That was never my intent."

Chloe settled beside Lucy, while Agnes took up a post behind the settee, tapping her foot. "I hope this will not take long. I am already behind on my program of study for today."

"No, it won't," Emma promised. "It is only something regarding Captain Trent's visit. He will likely be here late today or perhaps tomorrow, Christmas Eve, you know."

"Yes, we do know that already," Agnes said impatiently.

"What you don't know is the captain's purpose in coming here." Emma's voice wavered a little. She was making an effort to look too brave. A sudden terrible suspicion shot through Chloe.

"He's coming to say we cannot live here in his house anymore, to turn us all out of doors."

"No, Chloe dear. 'Tis nothing like that."

"Then what is it, Emmy?" Lucy demanded. "It is most unlike you to tease us so."

"It is just so difficult. I scarce know how to begin." A deep blush stained Emma's cheeks. "The truth is that Captain Trent is coming here to marry me."

Stunned silence met this announcement, the room going so deathly quiet, Emma was driven to repeat herself as if fearing they hadn't understood.

"The captain and I are going to be wed. Here in the village church."

"Well!" Lucy exclaimed. "Knock me down with a feather!"

Agnes frowned. "This does not seem logical, Emma. You have never met Captain Trent."

"But you know I have been corresponding with him on matters involving the estate and ... and such."

Chloe remained rigid, her shock every bit as great as when she had heard of her father's death. Her mind whirled, mostly with the image of Captain Trent that Agnes's words had recently conjured up. Chloe had a sudden horrific vision of Emma being dragged to the altar by some great, swarthy brute with gold rings in his ears, a cutlass clenched between his teeth.

"Oh, Emma!" she burst out with a deep gulp. "You can't! You mustn't."

"Of course she must." Lucy shot Chloe a look of deep scorn. "It is a very good match. The captain is exceedingly wealthy and of good family. Of course, there is no title, but"—she turned to Emma—"this is so much better than I ever hoped for you, Emma."

"Thank you, my dear," Emma said in dull tones.

"My heartiest congratulations, Em." Lucy rustled over to plant a kiss on Emma's cheek.

"Mine, too," Agnes said. Even at sixteen, she was still mystified as to why one would want to marry anyone. But she followed Lucy's example and went to give Emma a hug. But it seemed to Chloe Anne that it was mostly to her that Emma's soft brown eyes appealed, looking for approval. An approval Chloe couldn't give.

What was the matter with all of them—accepting Emma's dreadful decision as though it were something to rejoice in? Lucy lost no opportunity in racing back upstairs. She simply had to write her fashionable London friends, boast that she was about to acquire a brother-in-law of wealth and distinction. Agnes yawned and returned to her book.

But Chloe remained rooted upon the settee, unable to move. Any misery, any calamity that came upon the family, Emma was always the comforter. She had cradled Chloe all night long when the news of Papa had come. But Emma made no move to either seek or give solace now. She tried to skirt past Chloe, murmuring about something that needed her attention in the kitchens.

Chloe could not let her escape so easily. She clutched at her older sister's sleeve. "Oh, Emmy, why? Why are you doing this?"

"Well, as Lucy says, it ... it is an excellent match."

"As if you care for such stuff. This isn't right. You know it isn't. You are not in love with the captain."

"I am sure that, given time, I will learn—"

"No, you won't. Not when you are already in love with someone else."

Emma paled. "Chloe Anne, please."

But Chloe continued relentlessly. "You are in love with Mr. Henry. And he is in love with you."

59

"N-no, Chloe. You must never speak of such a thing again."

"Why not, when it is true?"

Emma looked positively stricken. "Have I been so terribly obvious, then, going about with my heart on my sleeve?"

"No, Emma, if anything, you conceal your feelings far too well. But I can hear it in the way you say his name, the way he speaks of you. And it was predicted, remember? That last Christmas Eve we spent with Papa, when I read your fortune in the lead. It said you would wed a clergyman."

"A silly children's game, Chloe Anne."

"Perhaps it was, but being in love is not. I have been expecting Mr. Henry to offer for you, oh, for ages."

A sad smile tipped Emma's lips. "Then you have little understanding of his character, my dear. He is a poor man, but very proud. While he can offer me so little and he is already burdened with the responsibility of his mother and younger brothers, he will never ask me to be his wife."

"Then you must wait. Surely something will happen. Perhaps he will get a better living or . . . or a rich uncle will die and leave him a fortune."

"We are a little too old to believe in fairy-tale endings, Chloe Anne."

"Perhaps so, but that is still no reason for you to rush into marriage with a stranger."

"I fear there is, Chloe. We are all under a deep obligation to Captain Trent. Not only did he permit us to continue living in his house, but I strongly suspect he has done more for us. Papa was returned to government service for only a few months. It is foolish to suppose he would have been paid such a handsome settlement. I suspect, nay, I am certain the captain has been supporting us with his own money."

"Oh, Emma. No!" Chloe exclaimed, much shocked.

"Yes, and even you must fully perceive how improper that is. He is not even that close a relative. It places us quite deeply in his debt. Since he has done me the honor of asking for my hand, it is clearly my duty to accept him."

Duty. Chloe winced. That was one of those disagreeable words that always applied to something vastly unpleasant. It did not at all fit Chloe Anne's romantic conception of what a bride's attitude toward her intended should be.

Yet Chloe saw the uselessness of further argument. Gentle Emma might be, but she could wax stubborn as well, especially when she was thoroughly convinced she was doing the right thing.

She would marry this captain in stoic fashion, be a good and faithful wife. Over the years, she would forbid herself to even think of Mr. Henry. But those moments would come, Chloe knew, when Emma would be unable to help it, and then her heart would break in silence.

Long after Emma had left her, Chloe sat alone in the parlor, feeling very bleak. The burden of that final responsibility Papa had laid upon her suddenly seemed very heavy, weighting down her heart.

Keep faith when there seems little reason to do so, believe that even the impossible can often be very possible. Be the Keeper of Dreams, Chloe Anne.

"How am I supposed to do that, Papa?" Chloe lamented softly. "When my sisters persist in dreaming of the wrong things."

There was Agnes, who seemed doomed to become

a hermit, going blind over her books. And Lucy, becoming so hard, almost mercenary.

Yet Chloe could scarce spare a thought for them right now. Emma was the one in most immediate danger. But how was one to rescue a sister when she refused to cooperate?

"You can't fling away your happiness in this fashion, Emma. I won't permit it." Yet even as Chloe formed this resolve, her heart misgave her a little. She would be putting herself into opposition against this unknown captain, who was fast assuming the dimensions of a bluebeard in her mind.

Well, she didn't care. Let him rattle his saber and bellow at her all he liked. If she had to move both heaven and earth to do so, she would find some way to prevent Emma's marriage to Captain William Trent.

Chapter 3

The winding drive came to an abrupt halt, and Windhaven Manor loomed out of the early-morning mist. With the fog so thick, it was as though one minute the house wasn't there and the next it was, in all its ramshackle splendor.

Leaning forward, Trent peered out the window of the carriage for the first glimpse of his inheritance. He stifled a soft groan. It was worse than anything he could have imagined. He knew that most great houses were the work of many generations, but he had never seen one that was such a positive horror of Georgian and Gothic revival. Far from the additions blending harmoniously, Windhaven simply looked as if one mad architect couldn't make up his mind.

The bailiff he had hired had warned Trent. In all his reports, Mr. Martin had found the house quite impossible. Of course, Trent meant to subject the place to a thorough inspection of his own, but he doubted he would waste much time or money on Windhaven. Very likely he would close up the house and seek to provide his new bride with some more suitable dwelling, perhaps closer to the port of London. Emma's sisters could continue to reside with her there until each of the girls had been married off in turn.

As the coach lurched to a halt before the front steps leading past the colonnade, Trent did not wait for the postilion to come to his aid. Tucking his cockaded hat beneath his arm, he shoved open the door and leapt down to the gravel path.

As he did so, the hilt of his dress sword tangled in his cloak. Trent straightened it, feeling more than a little foolish. He had given in to Doughty's cajolings and worn his uniform after all, although the Lord alone knew why. Perhaps because, although he was loath to admit it, he was experiencing just a hint of nervousness about meeting his bride. He was not attempting the role of a peacock, but surely it could do no harm to present himself in his best light, as an officer and a gentleman.

While Trent stretched his legs, a little cramped from all those hours stuffed into the coach, Doughty climbed down from the box where he had been riding with the coachman. One would have thought that by this time a groom or some sort of servant would have come scurrying forward to help with the horses, but there was no sign of anyone.

"Shall I start hauling down the baggage, Cap'n?" the steward asked.

"Belay that a moment, Mr. Doughty." Frowning, Trent stared up at the house, mantled in its early-morning stillness. An unnatural silence seemed to hang over the place, but then that might be owing to the mist. Fog had a way of lending an aura of unreality to things.

"I don't see no sign of Mr. Lathrop, sir," Doughty said, attempting the hopeless task of peering back down the drive. "Do you s'ppose we lost 'im?"

"Possibly, but Mr. Lathrop is more resourceful than he seems. I am sure he will catch up to us." All the same, Trent spared a glance in that direction himself. An excellent horseman, Charles had scorned making the journey closeted in the coach. An indifferent rider himself, Trent had not even been tempted to join him, especially not in this cold, damp weather.

Although certain his friend was all right, if Charles did not appear soon, Trent supposed he would have to go look for him. For the present, he turned back to his immediate problem, his astonishing lack of any kind of reception. Granted, he had pressed on a little hard, arriving a day earlier than expected. Still, his appearance should not take the household that much by surprise.

"Go knock on the door, Mr. Doughty," Trent commanded. "At least the butler must be up and stirring."

"Aye, aye, sir." Doughty bounded up the steps and beat an impatient tattoo with the brass door knocker. When moments passed and that drew no response, the steward used his brawny fist, hammering hard enough to set the portal atremble.

His efforts were greeted with nothing but that unrelenting silence. When the burly man raised his fist again, Trent called, "Hold, Mr. Doughty. This is of no avail. You have already pounded loud enough to wake the dead."

It was an unfortunate choice of words, for Doughty's eyes waxed large and round. "Aye, Cap'n, that's just what I was thinkin' meself. This be some sort o' ghost house."

"Don't be absurd," Trent snapped. That was all he needed, Doughty suffering from one of his attacks of superstition run rampant.

"D'ye want me to try peekin' in some o' the windows?" Doughty clearly made this offer with all the valor he could muster, but he swallowed deeply.

"Of course not," Trent said. "Go around back of the house and see if you can roust out a groom or stableboy. I shall go try one of the other doors."

"Aye, Cap'n." Doughty looked none too happy about it, but he shuffled off to obey.

Trent stalked back along the drive, gravel crunching beneath his boots. The noise sounded unnaturally loud, as noises were wont to do in fog. He spied a path winding around the side of the house and took it, thinking it might lead to a garden entrance or perhaps the kitchen door.

The path was thick with overgrown shrubberies, badly in want of a trimming. The sight of nature run wild only added to the house's air of desertion, of being lost to the enchantment of time.

Trent was not often given to harboring fancies, but he began to feel as if he had strayed into some strange dream, a dream in which he had only imagined Sir Phineas Waverly, his four daughters, and the betrothal to Miss Emma. Perhaps the mists would close and the house itself disappear in a minute.

Trent brought himself up short, disgusted with himself for entertaining such foolish thoughts. At the next turn in the path, he would chance upon someone, some logical explanation for why no one had come forth to greet him.

Yet what happened next seemed to defy all logic. One of the bushes at the corner of the house was seized with a violent fit of shaking. Then a laugh carried to Trent's ears, like the silvery tinkling of bells.

It was low, musical, and almost haunting. Trent started in spite of himself. He brought himself up short and called out in his best quarterdeck roar,

"Is someone hiding over there? Show yourself at once."

He would not have been surprised if he had received no answer, given the strangeness of everything else about this place. But the next second, a young girl skipped out onto the path. Although she was garbed in a long, green coat, Trent could tell that she was as slender and graceful as a sylph. Her hood was flung back, revealing masses of golden brown hair, tumbling in waves about a delicate face, an ivory complexion blushed with rose.

Because she came upon him as she did, so suddenly out of the mist, Trent was reminded of those legends his sailors wove on dark, lonely nights at watch. Legends of a nymph riding the ocean's foam, a lady of the sea, calling with her siren song, her arms outstretched. Trent himself had never been visited by such an apparition. Until now.

The girl halted a few feet away from him on the path and dropped a curtsy. "Good day to you, sir," she said simply.

It took Trent a moment to realize he was staring, frozen as though some spell had been cast upon him. He snapped himself out of it with a brisk shake.

"Good day, miss. . . ." He paused, subjecting the girl to a quick assessment, deciding that whoever she was, she could not be his Miss Emma. "Are you one of the daughters of this house?"

Before the girl could reply, a second figure seemed to dart out from nowhere. Erupting from behind the girl's skirts was a moppet of a child, a coarse woolen cap crushing her flyaway baby curls. She was bundled up in a thick coat that made her look round enough to roll.

Yet the urchin still managed to launch herself at Trent and fling her arms about his knees. He stiffened, considerably taken aback. His experience with small children was limited, but he followed one invariable formula. Admire their well-scrubbed appearance, give them a stern smile, and pat them on the head.

But he had never had one leeched to his leg before. Moreover, besides appearing grubby, with blueberry stains about her mouth, this babe looked fierce enough to take off his hand should he attempt to touch her.

"Kotcha, kotcha, kotcha," she called out in a singsong of triumph. "Bean'tu n'elf kin?"

Trent felt very much as though he had wandered into a strange land whose inhabitants spoke some Lilliputian language he could not comprehend.

"I am afraid I don't quite understand," he said.

The girl in the green coat broke into a trill of laughter. Her remarkable light blue eyes sparkled like sunshine on the water. "Peggety wants to know if you are the king of the elves," she said, amazingly able to translate the moppet's speech.

"Certainly not!" Trent told the child gruffly.

"Bean'tu kin o'ferries, 'en?" Peggety demanded, equally as gruff.

"Be not you the king of the fairies, then?" the young girl repeated.

"No!" Trent bent down to pry the child away, but Peggety had already released him with a look of disgust.

"C'mon, Klooey," she said, tugging at the older girl. "No ferries 'ere. 'Et's go back inner kittchin n'eat s'more pie."

With that, the child ambled off down the path, vanishing round the corner of the house. Trent almost reached out, fearing the girl would disappear as well.

But she lingered to apologize. "I am sorry if Peggety startled you, sir. We have been searching in the bushes for fairies all morning without success, and she has grown impatient."

"Upon my word!" Trent exclaimed. "Do you think that a proper game to play with the child, encouraging her to believe such nonsense?"

"Why not? We might actually turn up an elf or two."

"Of course you won't."

"But we could."

Trent raked the girl with an impatient stare. He realized the girl must be older than he had first imagined. Her lack of inches had deceived him, but the hinting of her curves did not. She must be eighteen, at the least.

"Aren't you a little old," he said sternly, "to be thinking such things as fairies really do exist?"

"Aren't you a little young to be so sure that they don't?"

Trent scowled. This absurd conversation was getting him nowhere. The young woman confounded him further by saying pleasantly, "You are a stranger to these parts, sir. Are you lost?"

"I didn't think so," he muttered. "But now I am not so sure. Is this Windhaven Manor?"

"Yes, certainly it is." She studied him thoughtfully, for the first time appearing to notice the cockaded hat tucked under his arm. Trent's cloak had shifted open enough to reveal the shaft of his sword and the gleam of his gold buttons.

The young lady went suddenly pale, her eyes widening in dismay.

"Oh, by my saints!" she whispered. "Bluebeard!"

"I beg your pardon?"

"N-nothing," she stammered. Friendly enough

only a moment ago, she now took a wary step backward. "Could you possibly be Captain Trent?"

"I could—that is, I am! And you are?"

"Chloe Anne."

This soft response conveyed nothing to Trent until he searched his memory. "Oh, you must be Miss Waverly's youngest sister."

"*Next* to the youngest," she said, drawing herself up a little. She started to offer her hand, withdrew it and curtsied again instead. "Welcome to Windhaven, Captain."

"Thank you, Miss Chloe. Though I cannot say it has proved to be much of a welcome so far. Do you realize that no one came to answer the front door when I knocked?"

"Oh? That is not surprising. Emma and Polly are likely in the kitchen with Old Meg. That's way at the back of the house. Lucy is still abed, and Agnes, when she is reading, would never bother herself about the door. And as for me, I was—"

"Beating the bushes for fairies with Peggety. Yes, I know."

The girl finally had the grace to blush.

Trent continued, "I wasn't aware there were any children upon the estate."

"There aren't. Peggety belongs to Sukey Green, who worked as a housemaid here until she married a sailor from Littledon. That's our village and near enough that Sukey still visits us. Our cook, Old Meg, makes the best possets, and Sukey is quite heavy with child and . . ."

Chloe Anne paused, looking a little self-conscious. "Er . . . that is, Lucy says that I should say Mrs. Green is 'in an interesting condition.' "

"Well, ah, yes. Ahem." Trent gave a deep cough. He was accustomed to hearing seamen swear with fluency and crack the most lewd of jests, but he felt oddly embarrassed to be discussing women "in interesting conditions." He made haste to turn the subject.

"I did find it strange when we knocked so hard and got no response. I thought we might at least have raised your butler."

The most enchanting dimple quivered in Chloe's cheek. "That would have been quite a feat, sir. Poor Giddings has been dead these many years, and we have never had another manservant. We always leave the front door unlatched during the day. Everyone hereabouts knows that."

"What! Leave the door unlatched so any mendicant might wander in! And what about thieves?"

"We have no thieves in this district. Besides, we have nothing to steal."

Trent's disapproval must have been obvious, for she tossed her head slightly. "We trust our neighbors enough to leave the door unlocked. That is just our way here, Captain." And she seemed to be defying him to change the custom, which Trent had every intention of doing.

He decided that he had been quite wrong to entertain any notion of Miss Chloe Anne resembling a sea sprite. No nymph would ever be possessed of such a stubborn little chin. But Trent was not seeking any confrontation at the moment.

He let the matter of the door pass, saying, "I did not mean to sound critical, Miss Chloe. I fear I am a little tired from my journey, and I would like to pay my respects to your sister."

"Which one? Oh, you must mean Emma." She looked a little glum as she reached this conclusion. "I suppose your sister has told you that—"

Chloe cut him off. "Yes, she told us all about *that*."

If Trent had expected any felicitations on his forthcoming marriage from Miss Chloe Anne, it was obvious he wasn't going to get them.

"I'll show you into the house now, shall I?" She brushed past him and set off down the path at an astonishing pace, leaving Trent to follow as he would.

She was a very odd girl, Trent decided as he strode after her. But he was too relieved at the prospect of finally being ushered into the house to give her abrupt behavior much further consideration.

Round the front of the house, it appeared that Doughty had managed to at least locate a groom. The young man was helping the steward unload the baggage. Chloe Anne paused to stare at the burly seaman with such fascination that Trent felt obliged to introduce him.

"This is my steward, Miss Chloe Anne. Mr. Doughty."

"Oh, he is much more what I had imagined that you—" Whatever she had been about to say, she gulped it back with a guilty look.

Burdened as he was by Trent's trunk, Doughty managed a bow of sorts and flashed his infamous grin. "Morning, miss."

After staring a moment more, Chloe smiled back, a most dazzling smile. Trent discovered that she had two dimples. He also reflected that she had not given him such a smile of welcome. Though he did not know why that should bother him, it did. He growled at Doughty to stop grinning and get the baggage stowed inside.

"And after that, snag hold of that groom and see where the deuce Mr. Lathrop has disappeared to!"

The event Chloe Anne had so dreaded had come to pass. The captain had arrived. Although she was ashamed to admit it and even felt it was a little wicked, she had been offering up silent prayers since Emma had made her announcement yesterday. Prayers that something might happen to keep Captain Trent's shadow from their door, some adverse wind, some change in his orders. Better yet, some change in his mind.

But those prayers must indeed have been wrong, for they had gone unanswered. Here was the captain, striding across Windhaven's threshold, and Chloe's acquaintance with him had not gotten off to the most auspicious beginning.

If she had only recognized him at once, she could have saved herself a deal of embarrassment. That was all Agnes's fault, spouting a bunch of nonsense about rum-soaked tyrants who bellowed and waved cat-o'-nine-tails.

Captain Trent did not in the least resemble the fierce sailor Chloe had been expecting. In fact, he appeared very much the gentleman, from his fine-chiseled features to the gleaming tips of his boots. She would not have taken him to be a seaman at all except for his deep tan and the slightly rolling gait to his walk.

When she ushered him into the drawing room, he glanced about him with a slight frown. Never had the flaws in the chamber seemed so glaring to Chloe, from the stain on the carpet to the splintered woodwork on the window.

Although the captain hadn't said a word, Chloe felt herself obliged to speak up, hating the defensive note in her own voice. "It's ... it's a well-proportioned room, isn't it? And if you look out that window over there, there is a lovely view."

"I am sure there is," the captain said politely. He stripped off his cape, and Chloe could not restrain a small gasp. He looked very much like a modern-day knight in his uniform, except that instead of the shine of armor, he had gold epaulets affixed to a pair of broad shoulders. The blue broadcloth jacket tapered to a trim waistline, a score of bright buttons drawing attention to the breadth of his chest.

Seeming a little self-conscious beneath Chloe's stare, Trent straightened his cuffs. "I suppose the uniform does look a little strange in a lady's drawing room," he said.

"Oh, no. You look very handsome. That is, *it* does. I mean the uniform—" She broke off, flushing, recollecting that this was the enemy she was admiring, the man who had come to Windhaven to take their Emmy away, to cut up all their peace.

The captain acknowledged her compliment with a fleeting smile. Chloe could not imagine why, but she had the distinct impression that she made him a trifle nervous. Perhaps he thought her quite mad after that business about the fairies.

She supposed she could try to offer some better explanation of her game with Peggety. The child lived in a tumbledown cottage at the edge of the village. She already knew too much of the grim realities of poverty. Let Emma knit her wool caps and Old Meg fill the babe with hot soup. Sometimes a child like that needed a good dose of peppermint drops and fairies as well. Chloe thought it her duty to provide it.

Yet as she stole a glance into the captain's wintery gray eyes, she doubted he would understand that. And if he could not understand about Peggety, how was Chloe ever to make him understand Emma's being in love with a poor clergyman?

Even though Trent's civilized appearance had proved somewhat of a relief, Chloe was as determined as ever to rescue her sister from a loveless match. But it was one thing to resolve such a thing, another to find a way to go about it.

Perhaps she could simply appeal to the captain's better nature. He looked like a reasonable man, and yet . . . He might not be the cutlass-bearing pirate of her imaginings, but he didn't seem especially approachable either.

As he waited for her sister, he stood before the fire, one fist held rigidly against the small of his back. After a time, he said, "I don't mean to trouble you, Miss Chloe, but I would appreciate it if you would go and inform Miss Waverly of my arrival."

"Certainly, Captain Trent." But Chloe felt reluctant to do so. It was foolish, she knew. As if she thought that by dallying she could postpone the inevitable meeting forever.

In any case, matters were taken out of her hands, for Emma appeared at the door of the drawing room herself.

"Chloe Anne, Polly told me that a carriage has just been pulled into the stable yard. Is it possible that Captain Trent . . ." When Emma saw the captain, her words trailed away. One hand fluttered first to her hair, then down to wrench off the soiled apron she wore. A deep blush stained her cheeks, and her lashes fluttered modestly downward. Despite her disheveled state, Emma had never looked prettier. The captain would never be persuaded to give Emma up now, Chloe thought gloomily.

However, Trent did not seem particularly bowled over by the sight of Emma. He summoned his stiff smile. "Miss Waverly, I believe."

Emma nodded, taking a few hesitant steps into the room, but Captain Trent was already crossing to her side. He made a smart bow, then took Emma's hand. After a slight hesitation, he carried it brusquely to his lips.

Chloe felt quite forgotten and miserably out of place. Perhaps she should leave the two of them alone, but she wasn't about to do so, not for all the fairy gold in the world.

Emma blushed more deeply and rather nervously retrieved her hand from him. "Captain Trent, welcome to Windhaven. I am so sorry I was not on hand to greet you."

"My fault entirely, ma'am, for arriving so far ahead of schedule. I hope my untimely arrival will not cause you any great inconvenience?"

"No, not at all. Such . . . such a delightful surprise. Now you will be here to share our Christmas Eve festivities. I have been up since daybreak helping our cook with the mince pies and currant jellies."

A look of horror crossed the captain's imperturbable features. "You have been working in the kitchen, ma'am?"

"Well, yes. You see, our cook is getting on in years, and we have but the one parlor maid."

"This is intolerable. I gave Mr. Martin strict instructions that this house should be run in shipshape fashion, all your comforts seen to."

Chloe piped up indignantly, "Our house is well run, Captain. Emma is an excellent housekeeper."

"I am sure she is, Miss Chloe. I did not mean to criticize. My point is that she should not have to be." He turned to Emma, saying earnestly, "Forgive me, my dear. I had no notion you had been turned into a galley slave."

"Hardly that, Captain," Emma protested with a laugh. "And, indeed, I have not minded the work. In fact, I rather enjoy—"

But clearly the captain was not listening to her. He paced off a few steps, his hands locked behind his back, his brow furrowed in concentration. "A house this size needs a proper staff. You should have a housekeeper, at least, a cook, several kitchen maids, a lady's maid for you, Miss Waverly, and another for your sisters, a butler, and several footmen."

Chloe bristled. Perhaps it would have been nice to have a few more servants, but none of them wanted to see their cozy Windhaven run on the formal lines of other great houses. She said, "It has always been our way, Captain, to manage just as we are."

"Some ways must change, Miss Chloe," Trent said. "I am deeply mortified. I fear that I owe all of you a great apology." He directed his gaze toward Emma. "I have neglected my responsibilities, leaving you and your sisters to struggle on alone in this vast barracks of a house."

Chloe stiffened. For someone who said he didn't mean to criticize, the captain had a habit of doing a good deal of it.

"What, pray, is wrong with our home?" Chloe asked.

"The captain's home, now," Emma gently told her.

Chloe was deeply chagrined at the reminder, the captain scarce appearing less so.

"No, hear now! None of that, ma'am. Without question, this is still your home as long as you wish."

For the first time, Chloe felt a little in charity with the captain.

"That is, if it is still fit to be anyone's home," he finished. "Perhaps you and your sisters would care to live closer to London."

Chloe's good feelings vanished.

"No, we wouldn't," she cried.

"Chloe!" Emma murmured, giving her a warning nudge. Then she said to the captain in accents of appalling meekness, "Of course, we shall do what you think best, Captain."

"Well, there is no need to decide anything immediately," Trent said. "I suppose I won't know the true extent of the disrepair at Windhaven until I have subjected the house to a thorough inspection myself."

To Chloe's horror, Emma replied, "Oh, Chloe Anne can help you with that. No one is more familiar with all of Windhaven's little nooks and crannies."

The captain did not seem much more delighted with the suggestion than Chloe did, but he said with a polite nod, "I should be vastly obliged to Miss Chloe."

That seemed to be settled, then, although Chloe felt sick at heart. What would the captain say when he had a look at those sagging timbers in the west wing? It would likely be all up with her beloved Windhaven. Captain Trent was fast proving to be even more of a threat to all their happiness than she had first imagined.

"Well," he said, briskly rubbing his hands. "It would seem we have a great deal to attend to, Miss Waverly. We must fix the exact time of our wedding. Then send your groom to fetch Mr. Martin to me. Sit down with your sisters and compose me a list of your more immediate needs. Miss Chloe, you will arrange a time at your earliest convenience for my house inspection."

"Aye, aye, Captain," Chloe said, snapping to attention, whipping off a sharp salute.

Captain Trent looked a little taken aback, and Emma was positively aghast at this impertinence. "Chloe!"

Chloe felt a surge of heat creep into her cheeks, but she compressed her lips in a stubborn line. "I am sorry. There is just something about Captain Trent that gives one an uncontrollable urge to salute."

"I seem to have that effect on a good many people," the captain said gravely but with a twinkle in his eye. It was the first glimmering of a sense of humor that Chloe had detected in the man, but she was in no mood to appreciate it.

"I fear I am too accustomed to rapping out my orders. You will have to be a little patient with me, Miss Chloe." He smiled at her then, but Chloe maintained a stony front.

"You must be tired from your journey, Captain," Emma said, stepping uneasily into the breach. "Do let me have Polly show you to your room."

In rather hasty fashion for the placid Emma, she fairly shooed the captain out of the parlor. When he was out of earshot, she turned back long enough to regard Chloe with mild reproof.

"Chloe, whatever has gotten into you? You were

quite rude to Captain Trent, not like yourself at all."

But she had no opportunity to scold further, for Lucy's voice could be heard in the distance, calling out for Emma. She slipped out of the room, leaving Chloe quite miserable, her eyes smarting with tears she stubbornly refused to shed.

What had gotten into *her*, Chloe thought. Only that Papa was gone, Windhaven was no longer theirs but owned by this scornful captain, and Emma was preparing to marry this stiff-necked stranger.

She fled the parlor and escaped to the sanctuary of her room. She sat brooding on the window seat, her knees tucked up to her chin. She turned over the little wooden statue of Saint Nicholas in her hands, frowning into the figure's solemn eyes.

"The patron and protector of all unmarried ladies," she grumbled. "Isn't it about time you started doing your job?"

Burying her head against her knees, Chloe wished for nothing except to be left alone, but it was not long before Agnes and Lucy came bursting in upon her.

Lucy seemed positively bubbling with excitement. "Oh, Chloe, what are you doing moping up here? Don't you know that Captain Trent has arrived and a friend of his has just turned up as well?"

Lucy gave Chloe no chance to reply, continuing in a breathless rush. "He is a Mr. Charles Lathrop, only an Honorable, but very charming. And the captain is quite handsome and so dashing in his uniform, those epaulets real gold. Not in the least the dunderheaded boor Agnes led us to expect."

"I was only describing a hypothetical captain," Agnes said with a superior sniff. "You girls really ought to learn the difference between theory and fact."

"Pooh," Lucy said. "You just can never admit when you are wrong."

"Well, I will say this much. I was astonished to find that the captain seemed possessed of much good sense." Agnes always sounded agreeably surprised to find that virtue present in any man.

"Good sense!" Chloe cried, unable to endure any more of this foolish chatter. "That shows all the more what you know. Captain Trent has not been in this house five minutes and he is already plotting to board up Windhaven and pack us all off to London."

But this dire announcement did not produce the effect Chloe had hoped.

"London." Lucy sighed ecstatically, and even Agnes looked thoughtful.

"Well, the city does have a good many circulating libraries," she remarked. "And only think of the bookshops!"

"Books!" Chloe nearly choked. She had just told Agnes they might be exiled from Windhaven, and her sister talked of books!

"Anyway," Lucy interrupted, "we are having tea early, Chloe, so Emma says you are to come down at once. We are planning quite a party for tonight. Now that we have some gentlemen present, we might even manage a little dancing."

And with that, Chloe's two sisters rushed out again, seeming quite oblivious to the fact that she had not moved a muscle to follow them.

As the door closed, she could hear Lucy teasing Agnes, "It is such a relief to discover that Captain Trent is not the bluebeard you said he would be."

"I never said anything like that!"

The sound of their quarrel faded down the hall. Chloe still made no move to bestir herself. Her two sisters' good spirits and unqualified approval of Captain Trent left her feeling alone and isolated. She might have known Lucy would be so silly as to be dazzled by a handsome man in a uniform, but Agnes! Chloe's most sensible of sisters! Even Agnes was singularly lacking in perception, unable to see the threat the captain posed to their happiness.

Maybe he wasn't any coarse, swearing brute, but as Chloe recalled his hard gray eyes, she thought darkly that soon they would all find out.

Bluebeard could come in many guises, even with a handsome profile and bright gold epaulets.

Chapter 4

Trent parted the draperies of wine-colored brocade that adorned his bedchamber window and watched the sun set. The bleak gardens and orchard below and the trees shorn of their foliage by winter looked all the better for having the mantle of night drawn over them.

The captain gave a restless sigh, the floorboards of the room seeming too solid. It usually took him several days to accustom himself to the absence of a deck rolling beneath his feet, to not constantly being obliged to make decisions, rap out commands.

He was not a man framed for leisure, and he already longed to be doing something. Going over accounts with the bailiff, inspecting the house, interviewing prospective servants—*anything*. But, of course, none of that was possible. It was Christmas Eve, with whatever sort of revelry that entailed.

Despite his disapproval, his bride-to-be was even now down in the kitchen, supervising the preparation of the evening meal. Until more help could be engaged, Trent conceded the necessity of it. But perhaps later, he could sit down with Emma and plan out the final arrangements for their wedding. That much, at least, could be accomplished today.

Letting the curtain fall, Trent stepped away from

the window. With the fading of daylight, the bed-chamber had descended into darkness despite the fire kindled on the hearth. Trent lit several of the tapers in a candelabra, the candlelight casting flickering shadows about the room.

The simplicity of the guest chamber pleased Trent. It was not quite as large as his cabin upon the *Gloriana*, but then he didn't have to share this room with a cannon either. The furnishing consisted of the old-fashioned bed hung with heavy curtains, a single wardrobe, and one wing-back chair drawn up near a tripod table laden with an oil lamp and several books. A dressing table stood near the door, a pier glass mounted above it in a plain wood frame.

Emma had selected this particular chamber for Trent's use. It was as though she already understood his tastes. He felt altogether satisfied with his choice of a bride. Emma was all that her letters had led him to believe: sensible, gentle, modest. And to add to that, she had turned out to be quite pretty as well.

Her sisters also met with his approval—at least, two of them did. He had been rather amused by the scholarly one, Agnes. At sixteen, one often imagined that one knew everything. Agnes was positively certain of it.

As for Miss Lucy, she was charming after the fashion of the reigning beauties Trent had met during his infrequent leaves in London. By the time they had finished afternoon tea, Charles already seemed quite smitten with her, and Lucy appeared nothing loath to encourage his admiration. As her guardian, Trent supposed he should frown upon such forwardness. But Charles was ever the gentleman, and for all her assumed sophistication, Miss

Lucy had an innocence about her as well. Trent meant to keep something of an eye upon the situation, but a little mild flirtation was not going to break the heart of either one of them.

The only sister who seemed calculated to give Trent any difficulty was Miss Chloe Anne. As Trent set the candelabra atop the dressing table, his brow knit in a puzzled frown. He didn't expect to meet with universal acclaim or even liking, yet this was the only time he could recollect anyone taking a pointed dislike to him on first sight.

As soon as she had realized who he was, Chloe had regarded him with a wariness and reproach that he sensed were unusual for her. It appeared far more natural for her eyes to sparkle the way they did when she had been hunting for fairies in the bushes.

Perhaps . . . It was not a comfortable supposition but one he was forced to entertain. Perhaps she held him responsible for her father dying upon his ship. Trent would not have blamed her or any of her sisters if they had harbored such a resentment. Yet somehow he did not fancy that was the cause of Chloe Anne's hostility. Sir Phineas's name had never even been mentioned.

No, Trent was certain it was something else about him that offended Chloe's sensibilities. He stared into the mirror, subjecting himself to a critical examination. He hoped that he was not vain, but he thought his features regular enough to please a lady. Maybe it was the uniform, and the fact he had made rather an ass of himself in the parlor earlier, handing out his orders.

He had to remember he was no longer prowling the deck of his ship. Perhaps shedding the uniform would help. Rapidly he undid the row of gold buttons and began to shrug out of the blue broadcloth jacket. He was wondering whether Miss Chloe might be more partial to tan or his gray-colored frock coat, when he brought himself up short.

What the deuce did it matter which she preferred? After all, he wasn't marrying *her*. Since when did he allow himself to become so unsettled by the disapproval of a mere slip of a girl? And yet in his own defense, he argued that Emma was obviously close to all her sisters, and so his future marital relations might be much more comfortable if he could coax Chloe Anne into tolerating him.

With this view in mind, he finished stripping off his uniform coat. The silk waistcoat and cravat followed, but before he began undoing the white duck-cloth breeches, Trent made an annoying discovery. His trunk stood perched in one corner, never unlocked, and Mr. Doughty was in possession of the key.

Scowling, Trent strode across the room and yanked open the door to send for his steward. But, alas, there was no sentry ready at hand to be sent scurrying at Trent's command. Nor could Trent bellow for Doughty at the top of his lungs as he would have liked to do.

He would be obliged to descend belowstairs and find the rogue for himself, likely out in the kitchen, impeding the cook's progress while he flirted with that pretty parlor maid. Smothering an oath, Trent stalked out of his bedchamber. He was halfway down the stairs when it occurred to him he was clad only in his breeches and shirt.

But hopefully the ladies were all closeted in their own rooms, busy with their toilettes. And Doughty, it seemed, was nearer at hand than he had supposed. Trent could hear that infernal whistling, and it was coming from the direction of the drawing room. What the blazes could Doughty be doing in there?

The drawing-room door had been left ajar, and as soon as Trent pushed it fully open, he spied his truant steward. Mr. Doughty stood before the fireplace, his burly arms stretched upward as he struggled to festoon some sort of greenery along the mantel.

"Mr. Doughty!" Trent snapped.

Doughty's whistled tune petered out in a startled squawk, much like a wrong note thunked out on a pipe organ. The seaman whipped around, attempting to salute, and nearly poked his eye out with a sprig of holly.

"Oh, er, Cap'n Trent, sir!"

"What the devil do you think you are doing there, man?"

"Decorating for Christmas, sir."

"And in the meantime, my trunk stands unpacked. I can't even get into it because you have the key."

"Sorry, Cap'n. I will be abovestairs in a moment, sir."

"You'll be abovestairs now, Mr. Doughty," Trent said. Gesturing toward the holly, he added, "And get that shrubbery back outside where it belongs."

"Begging your pardon, Captain Trent," a clear voice suddenly piped up.

For the first time, Trent realized someone else was present in the room. Turning, he saw Chloe Anne descending a ladder propped near the window, her hands likewise full of greenery. He felt a prickle of irritation. The girl had never come down to take tea, claiming she had a headache. But she certainly looked healthy enough, a delicate flush blooming in each cheek, her eyes bright and defensive as ever.

No sooner did her slippers touch the carpet than her chin came up, and she seemed ready to square off with him. "Pray do not be angry with Mr. Doughty, Captain. It was I who commandeered him to help with the decorating. We always place holly and evergreen about the parlor on Christmas Eve and leave it up until Twelfth Night."

"Twelfth Night!"

" 'Tis bad luck to do otherwise, Cap'n," Doughty assured him.

"It sounds like courting even worse luck to leave it up that long. In point of fact, downright hazardous. The evergreen in particular will become quite dry and brittle. One stray spark from the fire or a candle and this whole room could go up like kindling wood."

"I don't think such a dire occurrence likely, Captain," Chloe Anne said.

Didn't she? Trent grimaced. Mr. Doughty, while he awaited the outcome of this disagreement, was already trailing one garland perilously near the flames.

"At least keep that plaguey stuff away from the mantel. Mr. Doughty, take it down from there," Trent commanded in what he thought was a most reasonable tone.

But instead of Doughty's prompt "Aye, aye, sir," the fellow actually had the impudence to look to Chloe for confirmation of the order.

"Mr. Doughty!" Trent roared, justly incensed by this insubordination. He might endure the lady's hostility, but he'd be hanged if he would permit her to incite one of his seamen to mutiny.

Doughty had the prudence to react with prompt

obedience. He began yanking down the holly. With a cry of vexation, Chloe Anne started forward as though she would intervene. She glowered at Trent.

"We decorate the windows, the arch of the door, and the *fireplace*, sir. That is the way it has always been done here for ... for decades with the exception of last year."

Trent felt himself to be a patient man, but he was getting tired of Miss Chloe constantly telling him the way things had always been done at Windhaven.

"And why were you afflicted with a bout of good sense last year?" he asked harshly.

To his surprise, the color ebbed from her cheeks. It was like watching a sudden frost blight a rose garden.

"Because last year was our first Christmas without Papa. None of us felt much like ..." Her voice trailed off to a whisper, seeming unable to say any more. But she didn't have to. Trent already felt as if she had dealt him a blow to the stomach. He wished she had, rather than looking so pale, those long gold-tipped lashes unable to veil the unhappiness in her eyes.

"I am sorry," he began gruffly, but she was already shaking her head in rejection of his apology.

" 'Tis quite all right," she said. "Tear all the decorations down, Mr. Doughty. I daresay it is not important, and, after all, this is Captain Trent's house now."

She dropped the evergreen that she had been holding onto the settee and stalked back to the window, where she stood hugging herself, her profile averted from Trent's gaze.

Trent had never sworn at a woman, but Miss Chloe was bringing him dangerously close to it.

Blast the girl, he thought, for making him feel like some sort of ogre, a villain who snatched sweetmeats from babes. He hadn't meant to deny her all the decorations. He had simply been expressing a natural concern regarding the safety of these arrangements. But Chloe seemed determined to construe everything he said in its worst possible context. It was high time that he and this truculent young lady came to an understanding.

Placing his hands on his hips, he said to his steward, "You may go now, Mr. Doughty. I want a few words alone with Miss Chloe."

"Oh, no need to do that, sir." Doughty spoke anxiously. "Actually, it was my notion 'bout hangin' the greens. 'Deed it was, Cap'n. My notion completely."

"Mr. Doughty! I said you were dismissed."

The big seaman shuffled toward the door, but he took his time about it, his large brown eyes fixed upon Trent with reproach.

"Confound it, man," Trent said. "I am not planning to keelhaul the lady, only talk to her. Now be off with you."

"Aye, sir." Doughty shambled out as Trent fairly closed the door in his face.

With her back to the two men, Chloe heard Doughty's departure with dread, wishing it had been the captain instead. She had already spent a wretched afternoon alone in her room, racking her brain for ways to prevent Emma's marriage, coming up with nothing. It all seemed so hopeless, beyond her control.

Only recalling Papa's words, to believe that the impossible could be made possible, had managed to restore her flagging spirits, once more reaffirm her hope and resolve. When she had recalled it was

Christmas Eve, she had brightened even more at the thought of doing the decorations both she and her father had always loved. There could be a special magic in it, drawing her somehow closer to Papa this night, no matter how distant the heaven he inhabited.

Yet here was the odious captain finding a way to spoil that joy for her as well, with all his practical talk of dried-up evergreen and fire hazards, reminding her, whether he meant to or not, that Papa was truly gone. And Windhaven belonged to the captain now.

She heard his footfall behind her, approaching her retreat by the window. To her dismay, she felt tears filling her eyes, and she swiped at them in desperation. She hated to cry in front of a stranger, especially one so coldhearted as the captain. He would be bound to view any display of emotion with scorn.

"Mistress Waverly," he began sternly as he drew alongside of her. Yet when he caught sight of her face, he faltered. Chloe would not have thought it possible, but this man who had surely stood unflinching before the cannon fire of the entire French navy looked positively daunted. In a tone almost approaching panic, he said, "Chloe Anne. Here now! Belay those tears."

Unfortunately, this gruff command only made matters worse. Her tears spilled over to trickle down her cheeks. She mopped at them with the back of her hands, but to no great effect.

"I am s-sorry," she stammered. "I don't mean to be s-such a fool. It is only talking about the d-decorations and P-Papa. Christmas always meant s-so much." Her throat squeezed so tight, she could barely speak. "If you c-could just excuse me . . ."

"No, I cannot," Trent said.

Blindly, she turned to make for the door, but his solid frame blocked her retreat. He caught her face between his hands, his slightly calloused thumbs whisking away her tears with great efficiency. His touch was surprisingly gentle all the same.

"You never gave me the chance to finish what I was saying before," he chided. "I wasn't going to forbid the decorations. I'll help you hang the blasted things myself, on the mantel, the doors, wherever you want them. I'll even stick a sprig of holly in my hat, if only you will stop crying."

Chloe sniffed, wanting to thrust him away. But she was overcome by the ludicrous image his words painted, the captain fiercely sporting holly on the brim of his imposing military cockade. She hiccuped on a chuckle in spite of herself.

"That's better," he said. He stroked his thumbs across her face again, then cupped her chin and looked into her eyes as though defying any more tears to run his blockade. "You might have a little more forbearance for an old tar like me, Miss Chloe. I am not that familiar with these holiday customs. I have spent every Christmas since I can remember on the deck of a ship. Most times I forget what day it is unless one of my crew wishes me a happy Christmas."

"That is the saddest thing I have ever heard," Chloe cried, aghast. "How could one ever forget Christmas?"

"I fear the day's significance is not noted among my tide tables." Trent smiled, giving her damp cheek one final caress before allowing his hand to drop to his side.

"But surely when you were a child, you must

have celebrated," she said. "How old were you when you first put to sea?"

"Almost nine."

"Nine! And your mama and papa let you go?"

"My mother died when I was born, and my father was a quiet man who left my upbringing to my grandfather, Admiral Sefton. He obtained me a commission in the navy as soon as he could. It was a great honor to become a midshipman that young."

"I-I suppose it was," Chloe said doubtfully. The last thing she wanted to do was feel sympathy for Captain Trent, especially when the man seemed so sublimely unaware that anything was missing from his life, a wealth of Christmastide memories, the warmth of parental affection.

He appeared deeply embarrassed to have revealed this much about himself. She noticed that he had discarded his uniform. His shirt of thin white cambric outlined clearly the muscular play of his shoulders, the neck buttons undone enough to reveal a small vee of bronzed chest. Never had the captain appeared so vulnerable and at the same time so threateningly masculine.

Her heart hammered strangely and she would have felt more comfortable retreating, but the captain showed no sign of letting her go. He regarded her gravely, his eyes softening to the hue of mist.

"Miss Chloe Anne, we have had a great deal of misunderstanding between us. I fear that I can be abrupt at times. If I have ever hurt your feelings, I assure you it was unintentional. I would like us to be friends, but you seem to have decided this is not possible. Can you tell me why? What about me offends you?"

Chloe drew in a deep breath. Perhaps never again would the captain be so approachable. This at last was her opening to explain about Emma, an opportunity that must be handled with much delicacy and tact.

"I don't want you to marry my sister," she blurted out, then winced. So much for tact.

"Why not?" Trent asked, equally as blunt. "Do you find me that repulsive?"

"N-no. 'Tis only that you just met Emma today. You don't even know her except through her letters."

"That is true. I admit the circumstances surrounding our engagement are unique. But I often wonder: How much better acquainted are couples who have a more conventional courtship? They meet a few times at balls, dinner parties, walks in the park." Trent gave an expressive shrug. "I believe Emma and I have as good a chance of achieving a felicitous marriage as they do."

"Even if Emma is already in love with someone else?"

There now, Chloe Anne had said it. She braced herself for Trent's reaction—shock, disappointment, perhaps even anger. She was prepared for anything but how calmly he received her announcement.

"Oh, that!" he said, with a dismissive wave of his hand.

The shock, the disappointment, and the anger were all left to Chloe Anne to express. "You mean to say that you already knew? And you still mean to make Emma marry you!"

"Let us get one thing straight, Chloe Anne. I am not *making* Emma do anything. She accepted my proposal freely. She did inform me of a previous attachment to another young man, but circumstances rendered any marriage between them impossible. I honor your sister for her frankness. If she can put the past behind her, I see no reason not to do the same."

"Love cannot be so easily discarded, Captain, like it was last year's fashion. Emma still cares deeply for this other young man and—"

"She mentioned none of this to me," Trent interrupted. "Nor any desire to be released from our engagement."

"Of course she wouldn't, but—"

"Then don't you think you are taking a deal too much upon yourself to speak for her?"

"Well, I . . . I . . ." Chloe floundered, not able to argue that point as strongly as she would have liked.

"I understand that you are feeling a natural anxiety on your sister's behalf. But Emma is older, and, if you will excuse my saying so, a little wiser than you. I think you had best let Emma make her own decisions without trying to interfere."

His tone was kind but very final. He accompanied this speech with a condescending pat on her shoulder that made Chloe grit her teeth.

"Now I shall send Mr. Doughty back to help get these decorations up. I am glad we had this little talk, my dear. I am sure we understand each other far better now."

"But Captain Trent—" Chloe protested.

It was of no use. The man had already bowed and was moving toward the door. If he realized how Chloe seethed with frustration, he was determined to ignore it.

"Oh yes, I understand you perfectly," she muttered, waiting until the door clicked shut behind him before adding, *"Bluebeard!"*

* * *

Except for last Christmas, when her heart had yet been breaking for her father, Chloe could not remember a holiday that she had enjoyed less than this one. The infamous Captain Trent was to blame for that.

He raised no further objections to the manner of their celebrations at Windhaven. He even joined in after his own grave fashion, helping to haul in the Yule log, bussing Emma's cheek underneath the mistletoe with all due solemnity.

Not because he took any great joy in the customs, but because he had been told this was the proper way to celebrate on Christmas Eve. And so he did it with the same precision with which he must have charted his course at sea or carried out the Admiralty's orders.

No one but Chloe seemed to find anything lacking in him. He was courtesy itself and very attentive to Emma, just as a prospective bridegroom should be. But Chloe detected no real warmth in his manner, no true delight in Emma's company. Oh, it was wicked, wicked that he could think to marry their Emmy only out of some benighted sense of duty or propriety, when his heart held no tenderness for her. It scarce surprised Chloe that her plea for him to release Emma had fallen on deaf ears. Of course the captain would account love of no importance. He didn't even know what it was.

Chloe observed as much of this excruciatingly polite courtship as she could bear, then excused herself. She retired to bed earlier than she had any Christmas Eve since her childhood.

The next day, she dreaded attending services, seeing poor Mr. Henry's face when he obtained his first glimpse of Captain Trent. It was a cold, frost-hardened Christmas morning, with a chill wind whistling through the crevices of St. Andrew's Church.

Situated on their family's pew, Chloe huddled between Lucy and Agnes for warmth, Mr. Lathrop, Emma, and the captain seated at the other end. One would have thought so many bodies packed together would have generated some heat. The church was quite crowded, from the humblest villager to the squire and his lady sporting a new velvet bonnet.

Even Mr. Henry shivered a little as he mounted the pulpit to read out his lesson. He was better at it now than when he had first arrived two years ago. He didn't stammer nearly as much. Perhaps he would never be gifted with eloquence, but Chloe thought the innocence radiating from his face more than made up for any faltering, his eyes shining with a humble faith, a great love for the story he related, the birth of the Christ child with his message of hope and peace.

Despite the cold, Chloe was sorry when the services ended. She shrank from that moment to come when greetings would be exchanged in the vestibule. The entire parish was already buzzing about the presence of the handsome sea captain in their midst. Although Trent had not worn his uniform to church, Mr. Henry had to be aware of who he was and why he had come simply from the way the captain offered Emma his arm.

The moment Emma approached Mr. Henry seemed so poignant, Chloe wondered how her older sister could bear it. How wretched to be obliged to address the man one really loved as though he were the stranger. Yet no one could have detected any difference in Emma's cheerful smile as she complimented Mr. Henry on his sermon. One had to have heard it in her voice, which became just an octave softer, or noticed it in the quick way she excused herself to go pay her respects to Squire Daniel's lady.

Agnes, Lucy, and Lathrop had managed to escape to the waiting carriage. That left Chloe the awful task of introducing poor Mr. Henry to his successful rival.

There could have been no more painful contrast than Mr. Henry, in his mended robes, his face more earnest than handsome, and the captain, with his erect military bearing and striking profile.

A moment of complete despair flashed into Mr. Henry's eyes. But he was not the sort to slap his brow or even glower. After the barest hesitation, he offered his hand to Trent, saying, "Welcome to Saint Andrew's, Captain. We have all looked forward to meeting the new master of Windhaven."

"I thank you, sir. I hope I will not prove too much of a disappointment after Sir Phineas Waverly."

"He was a kindly soul, may God rest him. But I am sure you will be a worthy successor. And . . . and may I offer my felicitations on your marriage to Miss Waverly. You are a fortunate man."

Chloe thought she had never witnessed a more quiet heroism. Anyone who did not know Mr. Henry's secret would never have guessed what such a gallant speech must have cost him. It was obvious the captain didn't. He accepted the clergyman's congratulations with the sort of casual thanks he would have accorded any well-wisher.

On a sudden impulse, Chloe invited Mr. Henry to dine with them that day.

"You know you have always shared Christmas with us," she insisted.

"I-I don't know, Miss Chloe Anne. Your sister,

Miss Waverly, is surely not expecting another guest, and—"

"Nonsense. Emma would be delighted." Chloe continued to press the clergyman, being politely seconded in her efforts by the unsuspecting Captain Trent. When the flustered Mr. Henry accepted at last, Chloe scarce knew if she was being more kind or cruel. She only knew she could not permit Mr. Henry to give up on Emma so easily. She would wager that if their positions were reversed, Captain Trent would not permit himself to be robbed of the woman he loved. Yet that in itself was an absurd conjecture—to think of the captain being that desperately in love.

Having achieved her object with Mr. Henry, Chloe wriggled her numb toes inside her boots, impatient to be gone. But she had to linger a few moments more while Trent praised the vicar's sermon. She was astonished to hear him trade interpretations upon a passage of biblical text. As Trent escorted her to where the others waited at the carriage, Chloe didn't hesitate to say so.

"You surprise me, Captain, that you seem to know your Bible so well. I would have thought Sunday another one of those days forgotten in the navy. Is it marked down on your tide tables, then?"

"It is part of my duty to read out services to the men," Trent replied. "There are too many storm-ridden nights when faith in God is all a sailor has left to sustain him."

Chloe flushed a little at this grave response, feeling ashamed of her ill-natured question. But she still avoided being handed into the carriage by the captain.

Trent grimaced. Any doubts he had had that his talk with Chloe Anne had been other than a dismal failure were speedily put to rest. Not that he had entertained many. It had been obvious all of last evening that Chloe had determined not to accept him into her family.

And it was all because of her childish fancy that he was ruining Emma's life, separating her from her one true love. Chloe's conviction on this point was so strong, it began to give Trent pause himself.

He had spent much of his Christmas Eve narrowly observing his intended, looking for any sign her heart was breaking. But he had never known any lady in his life more placid or cheerful than Emma Waverly. Any desperate longings on her part had to be attributed to Chloe's romantic imagination.

But there seemed no way of convincing Chloe Anne of that. She continued to treat Trent to a degree of coldness all the more marked when contrasted to the warmth with which she greeted Mr. Henry when he joined them for Christmas Day dinner.

Chloe persisted in singing the man's praises to the entire company, deeply embarrassing the clergyman. Mr. Henry was so valiant, so generous, and so scholarly. Apparently, Trent thought irritably, the man was Aristotle, Francis of Assisi, and Saint George all rolled into one.

By the time they all sat down to dine, Trent began to entertain the unwelcome suspicion that Chloe Anne was infatuated with the young man. As her guardian, Trent would be obliged to inform her that he found Mr. Henry a most unsuitable match. Although at first Trent had though the vicar quite likable, he now began to detect numerous flaws in the man. Mr. Henry had a weak chin. He was too modest, too self-effacing.

He blushed like a woman during the main course of roast beef and pudding while Chloe continued to rattle on about his nobleness of spirit.

"I daresay you are quite tired, Mr. Henry." She directed a particularly sweet smile at Trent. "Dear Mr. Henry visits every poor parishioner at Christmas, makes sure they all have a log for their fire and a kettle of warm soup."

"Very creditable, I'm sure," Trent said, taking a sip of his wine, wondering why it should be so sour.

"Only my duty," the vicar mumbled.

"I do hope you found Sukey Green and little Peggety well?" Emma inquired anxiously. "I have been quite worried about them."

"They are as well as can be expected." Mr. Henry gave a slight cough of embarrassment. "I did wonder if a certain blessed event might take place today on Christmas and instructed the midwife to keep herself at the ready."

"Poor Mrs. Green," Lucy cooed. "It must be so hard to be in an interesting condition with one's husband so far away."

"Very imprudent of her, I call it," Agnes said, beckoning for her third helping of plum pudding. "I wonder why people that poor will persist in having so many children."

Chloe flushed with indignation. "Poor people have as much right to . . . to be as *interested* as anyone else."

This ingenuous remark set Lathrop off into a choking fit, and Trent himself was obliged to snatch up his napkin to hide his smile.

Chloe leveled an accusing stare down the length of the table at him. "I see no occasion for amusement, Captain. I fear Mrs. Green's problem is all the fault of your precious Admiralty."

"Is it, by Jove?" the irrepressible Lathrop called out. "To think I always fancied the Admiralty such a bunch of stuffy old men."

Lucy giggled, rapping Lathrop's wrist and crying fie upon him. Seeing both Emma and Mr. Henry appear much shocked, Trent frowned reprovingly at his friend.

As for Chloe Anne, she had turned a bright red. "What I meant was, the Admiralty is responsible for the Greens' poverty. Tom Green has sailed upon naval warships for nearly six years, yet he hardly ever receives his proper pay."

Trent frowned. "I will admit the navy is frequently lax in that regard. It is a difficulty I have experienced aboard my own ship."

Lathrop said warmly, "And a difficulty you have dealt with out of your own pocket. It is often Trent's custom, Miss Chloe, to pay his sailors' wages himself."

"Oh." Chloe looked momentarily nonplussed.

Trent was far too proud to allow the girl to strain herself, being obliged to think well of him on some score.

"It is only a matter of good policy to keep one's crew content. Mutiny must be avoided at all costs."

The cold speech would have served its purpose except unfortunately, at that moment, Mr. Doughty was passing through the dining room, helping Polly serve up the meal.

"Oh, aye, Cap'n." Doughty grinned. "I 'spect that's why you sent a deal of money to the bosun and gunners' widders and children. They be a fierce pack o' mutineers, them orphans."

"That will do, Mr. Doughty," Trent growled. He was mortified to discover that he became embarrassed as easily as Mr. Henry did.

"There must be a great deal of hardship involved in being a sailor," Emma remarked in her gentle accents.

"Amen to that," Doughty mumbled as he backed out of the room, his arms laden with empty plates.

Trent glowered at him before conceding, "I suppose it is not always pleasant aboard ship. One frequently contends with seasickness, storms, contaminated water supplies."

"How Papa must have hated it," Chloe said sadly.

"Perhaps," Trent said. "But I never knew Sir Phineas to make any complaint. After he gained his sea legs, he took quite an interest in the operation of the ship. Given time, I believe he could have—" Trent broke off, wanting to curse his own tongue. Time was obviously the one thing that had not been granted Sir Phineas. Trent's unfortunate remark seemed to have a sobering effect on the whole table. Even Charles shoved away his trifle, untasted.

"The letter you wrote informing us about Papa was so brief, Captain Trent." Chloe raised troubled eyes to his. "Can you not explain anything more about what happened?"

What had happened? Trent thought bleakly. A musket ball had happened. He avoided her gaze, taking refuge in his wineglass instead. As though caught in the sparkling liquid, painful images flickered before Trent's eyes—Sir Phineas lurching forward, the bright crimson stain pooling over the old man's chest.

Trent could never remember losing his sense of calm during battle until that moment. He had dropped to the deck, catching Sir Phineas in his arms, threatening him, cursing. Yet not one of his oaths could stay the old man's course a moment longer. There was nothing more humbling than death to remind a captain that he wasn't God, not even on the deck of his own ship.

Thrusting the memory away, Trent set down his wineglass with a sharp click. "This scarcely seems like anything to talk about on Christmas Day."

Chloe Anne started to protest, but she was gently shushed by Emma. Though she appeared far from satisfied, Chloe was obliged to subside. The meal was finished in an awkward silence.

Before long, the ladies retired to the drawing room. Although Trent managed to shrug off the lowering of spirits that discussing Sir Phineas had produced, he was not tempted to linger long over his port. He found it difficult to enjoy Mr. Henry's company, and Lathrop made his eagerness to rejoin Miss Lucy all too apparent.

As Trent followed the other two men into the drawing room, he felt in little humor for another evening spent in merrymaking, especially if he was obliged to watch Chloe fawn over Mr. Henry.

She was making such a fool of herself over the man, Trent longed to give her a brisk shake—that is, until something occurred to shed new light upon her motives.

Lathrop most charmingly begged the ladies for a little music.

"I am seized with the most uncontrollable desire to dance," he said, smiling at Lucy.

But Chloe Anne darted between them, dragging Lucy to the pianoforte. "Lucy must play for us," she said. "She does it so beautifully."

"Nonsense, Chloe Anne," Lucy cried, tugging her hand free, looking by no means pleased. "You know Emma plays far better than I."

"But Mr. Henry wants Emma to stand up with

him, don't you, sir?" Chloe appealed to the young clergyman.

"Well, I . . . I . . ." poor Mr. Henry stammered. And in that instant, comprehension flashed through Trent's mind.

Chloe Anne had not been throwing herself at the vicar's head all afternoon. Rather, she was endeavoring to toss the hapless fellow at Emma. Mr. Henry must be the man Chloe believed Emma adored, and she was desperately trying to thrust them together.

Yet all her innocent machinations were to no avail. Far from looking like star-crossed lovers, Emma and Mr. Henry merely seemed discomfited by these tactics.

Poor Chloe Anne. She all but wrung her hands as Emma lost no time in slipping behind the pianoforte and Mr. Henry asked Agnes to dance. Lucy paired off with Lathrop, and as the two couples began moving through the paces of a simple country dance, Chloe Anne was obliged to retreat to one side, looking mighty disconsolate.

Now that he perceived the truth of the matter, Trent could regard her disappointment with a kind of tender amusement. He even sympathized a little with her desire to secure Mr. Henry as a brother-in-law. Trent did not know how he had failed to do so before, but he now saw that Mr. Henry was a very likable fellow, possessed of great strength of character.

Chloe appeared so woebegone, Trent could not help making his way to her side.

"Come, Chloe Anne," he said, offering her his hand with a smile. "I would deem it a great honor if you would stand up with me."

"No, thank you," she bit out, the rejection sharp and unmistakably final.

There remained nothing for Trent to do but withdraw. With a stiff bow, he retreated, feeling remarkably like a man banished to darkness, cut off from the light.

Even the short time he had spent at Windhaven had been enough to make him aware of the role Chloe Anne played in her family. She was the warmth, the bright spirit that spread sunshine on the bleakest day. To everyone but him, that is, Trent thought bitterly.

Even Mr. Doughty basked in the rays of her approval. When the burly seaman entered the parlor, bringing in more logs, Chloe skipped to his side immediately. Soon she and Doughty were lost in conversation, the girl appearing to have completely forgotten Trent's existence.

In this the captain was quite mistaken, for Chloe Anne remained very much aware of where Trent stood, alone, his arms folded, distanced from the laughter, the dancing, the music, the circle of light spilling from the hearth.

She felt a stab of remorse. Something akin to hurt had flashed in Trent's eyes when she had refused his offer to dance, and she did so hate hurting anyone. Maybe she should have explained that she never danced if she could help it. Not only was she tone-deaf to the lilt of music, but she had a very poor sense of rhythm.

Yet when did Captain Trent ever trouble himself offering explanations? It distressed her, the way he had refused to discuss what had happened to her father aboard his ship. That, coupled with the captain's blind obstinacy about Emma, made Chloe feel as though she would never be able to like the man.

She thought she had been so clever in getting Mr. Henry to Windhaven, certain that having him so near would bring Emma to her senses. But all her plotting had come to nothing. There Emma sat at the pianoforte, over there Mr. Henry danced with the wrong sister. Both of them looked so determinedly cheerful, while Chloe knew they had to be absolutely miserable. It made her miserable just to watch them.

She forced her attention back to Mr. Doughty, taking refuge in the genial steward's company as he stoked the fire. He was so full of salty tales and marvelous lore. She drew up a stool, coaxing him to tell her once again how it was possible to raise up a strong wind from the depths of the ocean by having all the cabin boys whistle on deck. Chloe wagered that Captain Trent didn't know such things.

" 'Course one needs to be careful, miss, that the wind don't become a squall," Doughty said with a sage nod of his head. "There can be a deal of danger, stirring up spirits from the deep."

Chloe listened, entranced, until she noticed that Trent had moved closer. Although he seemed to be absorbed in watching the dancing, she could tell he had heard what Doughty was saying to her. The captain rolled his eyes in scornful fashion.

Perhaps she would give the man a sharp lesson in eavesdropping.

"Of course," she said. "We have always had our own spirits here at Windhaven."

"You never say so, miss." Doughty paused in his exertions with the fire to wipe beads of sweat from his brow. His eyes gleamed with interest.

"Oh yes, the ghosts of two sisters." Chloe watched the captain out of the corner of her eye to be sure that he was also listening. "They were the daughters of the cavalier who first built Windhaven Manor, sweet, lovely girls despite their poverty.

Legend has it that they were twins who loved each other dearly and never wanted to be separated. But one day a knight came to marry the elder and take her away."

"Sounds in the natural course o' things, miss."

"It might have been, except that the knight was a very wicked, coldhearted man who did not love the elder daughter at all."

To Chloe's satisfaction, the crease of a frown appeared upon Trent's brow.

Doughty scratched his head. "Beggin' yer pardon, miss, but that don't rightly make sense. If this lady was so poor, why else would that knight 'a wanted to marry her but out o' affection?"

"I daresay he had his own nefarious reasons. In any event, the wedding never took place, for rather than be so cruelly separated, the twin sisters went out to a cliff near here. Holding hands, they leapt into the sea."

"Seems a little drastic, miss. Wouldn't it have been a deal more prudent for the older girl just to have refused that knight?"

"They were desperate young women, Mr. Doughty," Chloe said solemnly, determined to ignore this gaping hole in her tale. "The two ladies vanished into the sea foam, but not forever."

Doughty leaned forward eagerly as Chloe dropped her voice in dramatic fashion. "On bleak winter nights, their spirits still walk this house, seaweed tangled in their blond tresses, their eyes burning fire, their pale lips moaning reproach, to drive out all unwelcome strangers from this house."

Chloe thought she heard Trent mutter a soft oath, but Doughty swallowed, his eyes fairly starting from their sockets, his side-whiskers seeming to bristle on end.

"Sometimes," Chloe continued, "You can even feel the brush of cold, silken fingers along the back of your neck—"

"That will do, Chloe Anne!" Trent rapped out. His sharp tone startled Doughty so badly, he nearly tumbled over into Chloe Anne's lap.

"Aieee, Cap'n," the steward said reproachfully. "What a turn ye gave me, bellowing out that way."

"I shall give you a turn worse than that if you don't take yourself off. I think you would be better employed elsewhere, Mr. Doughty."

"Aye, aye, sir." Still looking a little shaken, Doughty managed a salute. As he beat a hasty retreat, Chloe glanced up to where Trent loomed over her. She protested, "There was no need for you to be so short with him, Captain. We were only—"

"I know full well what you were doing," Trent said. "And I'll have no more of it. Mr. Doughty is superstitious enough. You don't need to frighten him out of what few wits he possesses with a pack of fabricated ghost stories."

"What makes you so sure I was making it all up?" Chloe asked sweetly. "Don't you believe in ghosts, Captain?"

"I certainly do not, young lady, and I would appreciate your not encouraging my steward to do so either."

Chloe found it more than a little annoying, Trent's manner of speaking to her as though she were a child. Entirely forgetting herself that she had completely made up the story of the two sisters, she eyed Trent with challenge.

"It just so happens I once saw the ghosts of those twin sisters myself. Does that surprise you?"

To her astonishment, Trent laughed. It was the first time Chloe recollected ever hearing him do so. The sound was deep, masculine, and thoroughly delightful. Or it would have been if Chloe had not felt so vexed with him.

He smiled, chucking her under the chin. "No, my dear," he said, his eyes alight with amusement. "Somehow your seeing ghosts doesn't surprise me at all."

At that moment, Trent's attention was claimed by Mr. Lathrop. The interest in dancing had palled, and the captain's help was required in setting up tables for whist.

After one final injunction against any more ghostly tales, Trent sauntered off, looking so unbearably smug, Chloe longed to heave the bolster from the settee at his head.

The man was always so insufferably sure of himself, Chloe thought angrily. He did not believe in fairies or love or spirits. Just what the blazes did he put faith in, then?

She shifted upon her stool and snatched up the poker, taking over Mr. Doughty's task of tending the fire. As she took several sharp pokes at the blazing logs, she set up a shower of sparks, and one flame leapt up in an eerie vapor of blue, red, and gold. Somehow the sight inspired a vague idea in her mind. Gradually the thought became clearer, a notion so dreadful she should not have entertained it, not even for a second. But she felt her lips curve into a mischievous smile.

Maybe there was nothing she could do about Trent's lack of faith in the wee folk or the magic of love. But after tonight . . . Chloe gave a soft laugh and hugged herself.

After tonight, maybe Captain William Trent would not be so infernally sure about the nonexistence of ghosts.

Chapter 5

The mantel clock chimed one minute past midnight, and another Christmas was gone. Trent felt a twinge of melancholy at its passing as though something precious had just slipped through his hands. Which was a deuced odd notion, for what he had told Chloe Anne was perfectly true. Until this year, he had ignored the existence of the day.

So why, then, should he feel saddened as this particular one was about to fade into memory? Maybe because he had never spent a Christmas in the midst of such warmth and gaiety before. The Waverly ladies were an affectionate family, given to much hugging and kissing beneath the mistletoe that spilled over to include anyone in their midst. Charles handled it with great aplomb, Mr. Henry also appearing solemnly accustomed. Since Trent had never had sisters, he found it a little embarrassing.

For too many years, there had only been his grandfather. Trent could never remember the gruff old admiral bending discipline enough to embrace him at Christmas or any other time. Affection had been understood but never spoken, to be glimpsed in the fierce gleam of pride beneath bushy gray brows, never felt in the touch of a hand.

But as this Christmas party drew to its close,

Trent found himself corralled beneath the kissing bough, being soundly kissed and wished a happy Christmas by Emma and all her sisters.

All but Chloe Anne, of course. She attempted to slip out of the drawing room, tugging herself free when Lucy caught at her hand.

"For shame, Chloe," she said. " 'Tis you who always insist upon having the mistletoe and you who always declared you wanted a brother. Well, here he is. You cannot mean to neglect him."

Trent felt discomfited in the extreme, especially as Chloe ducked her head. Hiding behind her sheen of hair, she mumbled something about "getting an infectious sore throat" and "not wishing the captain to take it from me."

"Well, I like that," Charles said, laughing. "You showed no such tender concern when you kissed me and poor Reverend Henry. I assure you, Miss Chloe, Trent has a stronger constitution than either of us."

But after bidding a hasty good night, Chloe was already fleeing toward the stairs. Her rejection of Trent was obvious enough to engender an awkward silence. Flustered, Emma turned to Trent to apologize for her sister.

"Chloe has been behaving so strangely. Perhaps all the excitement has wearied her."

Not the excitement, Trent thought. It was him that Chloe was wearied of. But he managed to smile at Emma and say that he did not regard Chloe Anne's brusque behavior in the least.

But he lied. He minded it very much. Later, as he sought out his own bedchamber, a curious mixture of hurt and anger lodged in his breast. He found himself wishing that he had stopped Chloe Anne, hauled her back under the mistletoe and—

And what? Made her bid him a merry Christmas

and kiss him? As if such a thing could ever be forced. No, Trent feared that for him such good wishes were as elusive as one of Chloe Anne's smiles, as the fairy folk she hunted in the shrubbery.

Trent retired to his room, but not to sleep. Besides the fact that Doughty was clumping about the chamber, insisting upon polishing Trent's boots at this late hour, Trent felt far too restless.

It might have been pardonable, he thought, for a man to be kept awake by dreamings of his intended. But he had difficulty even focusing Emma's image in his mind. It occurred to him that he did not even know what color her eyes were. He only knew that they weren't blue with gold-fringed lashes, eyes that could be most winsome when their possessor was smiling.

Chloe Anne again. He grimaced. Always Chloe Anne. He determined to drive the dratted girl out of his thoughts as swiftly as he meant to chase Doughty from his bedchamber. The seaman actually began a tentative whistling.

"Leave those boots till the morrow, Mr. Doughty," Trent said, shrugging a satin dressing gown over his nightshirt.

"But what about yer best gray coat, sir? It could use a good brushing."

"In the morning," Trent said firmly.

"Oh, er . . . aye, Cap'n." Doughty returned the frock coat to the wardrobe with great reluctance. Trent had not often had to complain that his steward was lax in his duties, but he had never known Doughty to be this assiduous either.

Even after he closed the wardrobe door, Doughty hovered, shifting from foot to foot.

"Anything else I can do for ye, Cap'n?"

"No, thank you, Mr. Doughty. I mean to read for a bit, then retire myself."

"Oh." Doughty nodded glumly. He took one shuffling step toward the door, then turned back eagerly. "I forgot to turn down the sheets for you, sir."

"I believe I can manage to lift my own coverlets, Mr. Doughty."

"Won't take but a moment, sir, and—"

"*Good night*, Mr. Doughty."

"What about me puttin' some more logs on the fire?"

"Go to bed, Doughty," Trent snapped.

"Aye, sir," Doughty said, looking quite crestfallen. His boots appeared weighted with lead, for all the faster he moved to obey Trent's command.

What the deuce was the matter with the man? Trent wondered. He almost behaved as though he were afraid to retire to his own bed.

Indeed, as Doughty reached for the brass knob, his huge hand did tremble a little. Anyone would think from the way he rolled his eyes that he expected to find something horrible on the other side of that door, something like a—

Trent stiffened with sudden comprehension. He forced back a laugh, his humor tempered with vexation.

"Mr. Doughty, I promise you, no matter what Miss Chloe Anne might say to the contrary, you are in no peril of being visited by spirits tonight."

" 'Course not, sir." Doughty flushed a bright red. "Such a notion never entered my head, Cap'n." Yet for all his bluster, he nervously licked his lips. "But that Miss Chloe, she do tell a mighty convincin' tale, don't she, sir?"

"Convincing?" Trent scoffed. "The ghost of one

dead woman sounds like nonsense enough, but twins!"

"There be stranger things, Cap'n. One night, when I was keepin' watch with the bosun up on deck, we seen—"

"Would that be the time I had to have the bosun flogged for breaking into the rum ration?"

"No, sir," Doughty said indignantly. "Leastwise, I don't think so. In any event, I saw it, too: the shape of a phantom bird. And I was as sober as the ship's surgeon."

"Considering some of the ship's surgeons I have known, that is hardly any recommendation."

"But, Cap'n, I'm only tryin' to tell you spirits can—"

"Enough of this folly, Mr. Doughty. You will retire at once. If you are that alarmed, draw the covers up over your head. It is a well-known fact that ghosts never disturb a man hiding under a counterpane."

"It is?"

Doughty's credulous expression snapped the last of Trent's patience. He was beginning to fear he was going to have to take the burly seaman by the hand and actually tuck him into bed. Crossing the room, he swung open the door and thrust Doughty through it, bidding the man a firm good night. Only when the steward had gone did Trent shake his head with a wry amusement. He could scarce believe it.

Doughty was bold enough to face half a dozen French pirates with their sabers drawn but shook in his boots at the mere imaginings conjured up by a slip of a girl. Trent supposed he had better repeat his lecture to Chloe Anne tomorrow just to be certain she understood. Definitely no more ghost tales.

She wouldn't be pleased, but Trent doubted he could do anything to make her dislike him more than she already did.

With Doughty gone, Trent breathed a sigh of relief, drinking in the silence of his room. Charles, sociable creature that he was, might deplore the early hours they kept here at Windhaven, but Trent was grateful for a little solitude.

Reading was a pleasure he was seldom able to indulge in, and he moved eagerly toward the small stack of books left upon the tripod table. But as he examined the titles, he grimaced. Walpole's *Castle of Otranto*. *Songs of Innocence* by William Blake. Samuel Johnson's *Lives of the Poets*.

He had not expected to find the manuals on navigation and military tactics that were his usual fare. But he had hoped for at least a volume of logic or history. He should have reflected that the books must have been selected and left here for him by Emma. A lady would have no notion as to a man's tastes.

Since he still did not feel at all tired, he settled back in the chair and reached for *Lives of the Poets*. He supposed it was a history of sorts.

But as he flipped open the cover, his fingers stilled, going no further than the flyleaf. His gaze settled upon the inked scrawl that sketched out the name of the volume's previous owner.

Sir Phineas Waverly.

Trent checked the other two books. They were marked the same. Comprehension slowly broke over him. The books had not been placed here for his particular use. They had been left by this chamber's previous occupant.

Dolt that he was, he should have realized sooner that this had been Sir Phineas's room. But Emma had said nothing, and Trent had imagined that the master bedchamber would have been much large and grander.

If he had been thinking more clearly, he would have known at once. This small room with its simple furnishings fit so well with what Trent remembered of the gentle old man. He could easily picture Sir Phineas sitting here by the fire, his spectacles perched upon his nose, reading until the candle guttered low in its socket.

Carefully, Trent closed the book he held and returned it to the table, feeling very much an intruder, as though he had no right to be touching the volume, no right to even be in this room.

Perhaps he had been wrong to be so adamant with Mr. Doughty, he thought bleakly. It would seem that Windhaven had its hauntings after all.

This curious notion had no sooner passed through his mind than Trent was startled by a muffled cry that caused the hair on the back of his neck to prickle. He jumped as the next moment his bedchamber door crashed open.

Doughty burst into the room, looking pale enough to be a ghost himself. He slammed the door behind him and leaned up against it as though a thousand devils lurked beyond, ready to break down the portal.

Given such an unpleasant jolt, Trent jerked angrily to his feet. "Now, what the devil . . ."

"Aieee, Cap'n," Doughty wheezed, his chest heaving. He could scarce get his words out for his terror. "S-seen it. I s-seen it."

"Seen what? Your own shadow?"

Doughty lurched across the room to catch at the sleeve of Trent's robe. "S-seen her. *Her.* One o' them ghost twins. I just t-took one more peek into the hall afore I went to sleep. J-just to be sure it was safe. An' there she was! Liftin' her arms and moanin'!"

"Damnation, man!" Trent attempted to shake off Doughty's grasping fingers. "You must have had some sort of nightmare. Now I have endured about enough—"

He broke off as a strange sound carried to his ears. A sound like a low groan. He knew it hadn't come from Doughty. The seaman was panting so hard, he could barely whisper. Besides, the sound was soft, like a woman's voice, muffled as though it came from the hallway beyond.

Even as Trent frowned at his closed door, he thought he saw a shadow pass over the crack at the bottom. The knob rattled, then slowly began to turn.

"Lord above protect us!" Doughty squeaked. He ducked behind Trent as though hoping to hide his hulking frame. "You should'a never broke that statue of Saint Nicholas, Cap'n," he told Trent reproachfully.

"Quiet!" Trent hissed, his gaze fixed intently upon the door, which now seemed to be creaking open of its own accord. He would have stridden forward and gotten to the bottom of this nonsense at once if Doughty had not maintained such a death grip on his arm.

"Who the deuce is out there?" he roared. "Show yourself."

"No, please don't," Doughty quavered.

Outside in the corridor, upon hearing Trent's bellow, the ghost herself was having second thoughts about the wisdom of her actions. The white lead paint she had smeared over her face was making Chloe Anne itch dreadfully, and the gown of the cavalier's lady she had fetched from the trunk in the garret smelled horribly musty.

But she had come too far to retreat now. Her pulse hammering, she steadied the wax taper she held and stepped forward until she stood framed in the threshold. The glow of the candle flame caused the veil draped over her face to take on an eerie translucence.

The effect must have been remarkable, for even Captain Trent appeared transfixed at the sight of her. Taking heart from his wide-eyed stare, Chloe Anne managed to summon up another piteous moan, well remembered from those days of childhood toothaches.

"Go away!" she cried out. "Leave this house!"

"Y-yes, ma'am," Doughty stammered. Trent stood, rigid as though he had been turned to stone.

Chloe inhaled deeply to give vent to another awful wail. That proved a great mistake, as she took too deep a breath of age-old dust particles clinging to the gown.

"Leave this—Oh, ah—ah—" She crinkled her nose, trying to fight the tickling sensation to no avail. She gave vent to a series of violent sneezes, which extinguished her candle. The flame snuffed out in a tiny trail of smoke.

Through watery eyes and the layers of her veil, she could see Trent coming to life. A dark look crossed his handsome features as he struggled to break free of Mr. Doughty's grasp.

A prudent ghost always knows when it is time to vanish. Turning, Chloe took to her heels and fled as quickly as she was able in the semidarkness of the hall, hampered by the stiff brocade skirts of the old-fashioned gown she wore.

It had been her intent at the conclusion of her

performance to disappear down the corridor and through the door that led to the servants' stairs in the west wing, the unused older portion of the house.

But she had meant to glide away majestically, mysteriously, not skittering, bumping into the walls like a half-blind mouse. She banged up against a fragile hall table, overturning it, sending a Wedgwood vase crashing to the floor.

But she scarce paused as she heard an oath, the sound of a footfall behind her. Someone was coming after her, and she didn't need to turn around to know who it was.

Scrambling madly, fighting both veil and skirts, she hurled herself down the hall. Locating the door at the end, she seized the handle and pushed. Unused for so long, the blasted thing stuck. Chloe put her shoulder to it and shoved, but she only managed to thrust it partly open when she was seized roughly about the waist.

This would have been the moment for a good bloodcurdling scream, but Chloe was too breathless to manage it. She pounded wildly at the arms banding her with a grip of iron.

"Let me go," she gasped. "What kind of fool would chase after a ghost?"

"Oh, stop your nonsense, Chloe Anne," Trent said. Still holding her tight, he freed one hand enough to wrench back her veil.

Moonlight filtering through the oriel window enabled her to see clearly the anger glittering in his eyes, the hard set to his jaw.

"What the devil do you think you are playing at—" he started to demand, but he was obliged to break off the furious scolding.

Sounds from the other end of the corridor, doors

opening, and voices calling told Chloe Anne that the rest of the household had been aroused. She could just hear Lucy's frightened cry.

"Emma, what was that crash?"

"I don't know, my dear. I was about to find out."

"Never fear, ma'am," Lathrop's sleepy voice called out. "I will investigate."

Chloe's heart sank. She knew that in another moment they would all be spilling into the hallway, demanding explanations. She had a lowering vision of how ridiculous she was going to appear when the lamps were lit. Bad enough that Trent had caught her, but whatever would she say to her eldest sister? Emma was going to be so shocked by this prank, so disappointed in her.

"Oh, please," Chloe whispered, wishing the walls could just open up and swallow her.

Her plea came involuntarily. She did not really expect it to be heeded, let alone answered. Therefore, she was startled when Trent suddenly released her. Forcing the door further open, he thrust her onto the darkened landing beyond.

"Stay here and be quiet," he commanded. "Don't you stir so much as a step."

Chloe was too astonished to think of doing otherwise. Besides, when Trent pulled the door closed, without her candle, she was left in unrelenting darkness. Shivering in the draft that wafted up the narrow stairwell, Chloe pressed close to the door, trying anxiously to detect what was transpiring on the other side.

The door was so thick, she could not hear well, only enough to guess at what was taking place. The high-pitched voices of Emma and Lucy and the deeper one of Mr. Lathrop all seemed to be questioning. Thank goodness Agnes was such a sound sleeper, capable of dozing on even if the roof had collapsed upon her. If she had joined the group in the corridor, Chloe Anne's absence would surely have been noted.

As it was, Captain Trent was able to convince everyone that Mr. Doughty had merely been sleepwalking, suffering from the effects of a nightmare. Poor Doughty sounded distraught enough to make this quite believable, his jabbering about a ghost all but incoherent.

Chloe heard Trent ordering the steward and everyone else back to their beds. After what seemed an eternity, she caught the sound of doors closing, the household once more settling to silence.

Leaning up against the door, Chloe breathed a sigh of relief. Much as she hated it, she had to feel somewhat grateful to Trent for rescuing her from the embarrassment and full consequences of her folly. When she heard the thud of his footfall, she quickly stepped back from the door, shrinking against the wall.

He swung the door open, the light from the candle he held momentarily blinding her. "Chloe Anne? Oh, there you are."

She held up one hand protectively before her eyes. She realized that the makeup that had appeared so sinister in the shadows must look downright silly in the light. She hardly knew what to say to Trent.

"Captain, I . . . I . . ." she began.

But he ignored her halting efforts, saying in clipped tones, "You will go remove that white muck from your face, then meet me belowstairs in the drawing room. If you do not come, I will fetch you. We needs must talk."

Chloe slowly lowered her hand, her vision adjusting enough to note the inflexible lines of his face, the hard martial light in the captain's eyes. Spinning on his heel, he marched away, and Chloe felt a tremor course through her.

It appeared that she had escaped nothing. The consequences of her little charade were yet to come.

Nearly a quarter of an hour later, Chloe descended the dark, silent stairs, heading for the parlor. The stiff brocade of the ancient gown yet rustled about her, but her face had been thoroughly cleansed, damp tendrils of her hair clinging to her cheeks from the vigorous scrubbing.

As she approached the drawing room, her heart seemed to be pounding in her throat. She thought she knew how an officer must feel on his way to be court-martialed. Through the open doorway, she could see her solitary judge.

Trent stood poised, awaiting her entrance, his arms locked rigidly behind his back. He had rekindled the fire on the hearth, and the leaping flames behind him cast his shadow, a giant, looming specter up one wall. Chloe stepped into the room, gathering what tatters remained of her dignity and defiance.

She presented herself before him, chin held high, saying nothing, waiting for him to speak first. He subjected her to a long, grim silence, the weight of a most awful stare. Chloe imagined this must be the method Trent used aboard his ship when he was attempting to intimidate some insubordinate seaman. It worked wonderfully well, she thought miserably.

At last he rapped out, "You have five minutes, milady, to give me one good reason why I should not bend you over my knee and take a switch to you."

Although Chloe flinched, she said, "I cannot give you one. At least not any reason you would understand."

"I will grant you that Mr. Doughty is not a fellow of great intelligence. He is a simple but good-natured man. I thought you had far more regard for him than to prey upon his superstitions. Was it that amusing to terrify him half out of his wits?"

"I never meant to do that. I thought he would be asleep in his own room. I did not intend for anyone to see me except for . . . for . . ."

"Except for me?" Trent finished when she hesitated.

The answer was so obvious, Chloe did not answer, merely setting her lips into a stony line.

"I see," Trent said. "It was only me you hoped to scare senseless."

He stalked closer. Her every impulse called out to her to retreat, but she forced herself to stand her ground. His fingers flicked contemptuously against one of the balloonlike sleeves of her gown. "Did you really think you could frighten me with this ridiculous masquerade? What did you hope to gain? Did you actually believe you could drive me from this house by pretending to be a ghost and moaning 'Go away!'?"

"I don't know what I believed." Tears of misery and shame stung her eyes. "You made me so desperate that I think I would have tried anything to be rid of you, to send you back to your wretched ship."

Chloe was a little appalled at herself as she blurted this out. But there was no recalling the blunt words. She tensed, awaiting Trent's answering flash of anger.

But he spoke quietly, bitterly. "At this moment,

you don't know how happy I would be to oblige you, ma'am. I wish the devil I was back aboard the *Gloriana*, where I don't have to deal with—" He broke off, raking his hand back through his hair, the gesture rife with frustration. "Go back to your bed, Chloe Anne. This discussion is useless."

He strode away from her, leaning one arm up against the mantel, his profile lost in shadow as he stared into the dying embers of the fire. It took Chloe a moment to comprehend that he was dismissing her. She should have felt relief, taken to her heels at once.

But she could scarce do so, not when she was under some obligation to the man. She cleared her throat. The words were the most difficult she had ever had to say, but somehow she got them out.

"Th-thank you for not letting the others find out about what I tried to do. Emma would have been so angry with me."

"This may be hard for you to realize, Chloe Anne, but I did not come here intending to sow discord between you and your sister."

"No? Well, thank you anyway."

She had expressed her gratitude. She supposed she was free to go now. Yet something held her to the spot. Perhaps it was the glimpse she attained of Trent's face. His anger had drained away, leaving him looking inexpressibly weary and strangely hopeless.

He was no longer demanding any explanations, and yet somehow she felt driven to explain. She took a timid step closer. "It is not that I bear you any ill will in particular, Captain," she said. "I would want to chase away any suitor who came to claim Emma except for Mr. Henry. You see, when

Papa went away, he told me to take care of the others. To be the Keeper of their Dreams."

"*Their* dreams, Chloe? Or the ones you think they should be having?"

"Well, I . . . I . . ." This pointed question gave her pause, making Chloe a little uncertain of her position.

"With great patience I endured watching you thrust Mr. Henry and Emma together. I even tried to observe her more closely on the chance you might be right." Trent shook his head. "I saw nothing but politeness and a little embarrassment."

"Emma is very good at concealing her feelings," Chloe faltered. So good, in fact, there were times when even her own sister did not feel quite so sure she understood Emma.

"I can see why you would prefer Mr. Henry as a brother-in-law," Trent said. "He is a very good man, a description that I fear cannot be applied to me. I have been called a hard man, relentless, aloof—all those things that make for a disciplined officer but not a very congenial companion.

"But there is one advantage to Emma's marrying me, Miss Chloe." He straightened, giving her a rueful smile. "I won't be around that much to plague you. This time next Christmas, I will be back aboard ship, keeping my solitary watch. You might have reflected on that and tried being a little kinder."

His words stung Chloe more than anything else he could have said. It was the first time anyone had ever accused her of being cruel. But then, she also suspected, it was the first time Captain Trent had ever asked anyone for kindness.

"I am sorry," she said. "It's just that everything has changed so. Nothing has turned out the way I ever thought it would be. We ... we were all so happy here before Papa went away. Then one terrible day, your letter came saying my father was dead. It was so hard."

"I understand," he said quietly. "Far better than you realize. I was but ten years old when the admiral summoned me to his cabin to inform me of my own father's death. He read the dispatch to me and expressed his condolences. I saluted and returned to my duties."

"You were given no time to weep?"

"It was my turn on watch. I was lucky, though. There was a storm. When the sea is driving spray over the side, one kind of salt droplets on a man's face very much resembles another."

He spoke without emotion, but his eyes clouded with the memory, and for one moment, Chloe no longer saw a man but glimpsed a ten-year-old boy, trying valiantly to conceal his grief from his mates.

Scarce realizing what she did, Chloe slipped her fingers into his. He raised her hand, looking wonderingly at it for a moment. Then, with a heavy sigh, he released it.

"I suppose what you really want to hear is about your father, not mine. I should have told you sooner, but you already disliked me so intensely."

Squaring his jaw, he said, "Sir Phineas died trying to save my life."

He waited for her reaction. When she said nothing, he continued, "The French war ship ... was so close. It seemed they would be attempting a boarding any moment. I was already bleeding from a wound to the shoulder. Sir Phineas was struggling across the deck, coming to help me, I think. I tried to warn him to go back."

Trent sighed. "A sharpshooter from the other

deck took aim, most likely at my uniform. But as he fired, your father stepped forward and . . . and you know the rest.

"Now you may hate me without compunction. You know exactly how I was the cause of your father's death."

He started to walk away from her, but not before she glimpsed the pain in his eyes and had an inkling of the burden of guilt he must have carried for far too long.

She touched his hand again, saying gently, "I only know one thing—that you are a man whose life my father must have believed was worth saving."

He flashed her a look of disbelief and such grateful astonishment that it tugged at Chloe's heart. Although she realized how difficult this was for him, she could not help asking, "Do you think it was very painful? Did my father suffer for long?"

"No, the end came very quickly, and such a look of peace stole over him, I shall never forget it. He seemed to stare beyond me at the last and whispered a name. It sounded like Maria."

"Did he?" Chloe raised her head. She looked almost radiant. "That's all right, then."

"It is?" he asked, thoroughly bewildered.

"Yes, don't you see? Maria was my mother's name. She came for him." Her bright expression momentarily dimmed. "If only we could have brought his body back to rest beside her in the churchyard, where he belonged. That was the hardest thing of all, to think of Papa being tossed into the cold, cruel sea."

"Do you think so?" Trent said. "Myself, I have more of a fear of being buried beneath the hard, unfeeling earth. I would much rather be lowered into the arms of the lady of the sea."

"The lady?"

"Yes. It is a fancy that sailors often have, perceiving the sea as a woman."

"Truly? What does she look like?"

"Well, she looks different to different sailors."

"What does she look like to you?" Chloe persisted, clearly fascinated by anything hinting of legend.

"I never really thought about it, but I suppose she would have delicate features, long flowing hair, and eyes the color of . . ."

He found himself staring directly into Chloe's wide blue eyes.

"Yes?" she prompted.

"And . . . and what a great deal of nonsense you can coax a man into talking, Chloe Anne." He gave a quick laugh. "You will have me as superstitious as Doughty in a minute."

"But no more ghosts, I promise." She favored him with a sudden shy smile. "I am sorry, Captain, about everything, how horrid I have been ever since you first came. I really would be glad to have you for a brother if only I could be sure . . ." She paused, giving her head a rueful shake as though determining not to open any old quarrels. "But it is very difficult when you have three sisters and all of you are so close, and a gentleman comes to take one away."

"You will feel differently when it is your turn."

"I fear that will happen only in my dreams. I am not as clever as Agnes or as beautiful as Lucy."

"No," he said slowly. "And yet you have one of those winsome faces. The kind that must have sent knights of old out on quests to slay dragons."

She blushed prettily. "Pooh. Now you are indeed

talking nonsense, Captain, and this time it isn't my fault."

"If we are indeed going to be friends, I wish you would call me something besides Captain."

"All right," she said, and then with a soft hesitation, "Will."

He had meant for her to call him Trent, as his friends did, as his grandfather used to. No one had ever addressed him as William, let alone Will. But he didn't correct her, the sound of that single syllable on her lips strangely sweet.

When they were on the verge of retiring from the parlor, she startled him by standing on tiptoe and suddenly kissing his cheek, her lips warm, whispering perilously close to the corner of his mouth.

Chloe must have perceived his astounded expression, for she pointed merrily upward. "The mistletoe," she said. "Merry Christmas, Will."

"Merry Christmas, Chloe Anne," he replied gravely.

She left him then, making her way up the stairs, smothering a tiny yawn. After such a night, things had a way of working out most strangely, he thought, as he watched his newest sister vanish into the darkness.

There was only one problem. He touched his hand to where he yet seemed to feel the sweetness of her kiss. For one moment there, when her lips had grazed so near his own, his impulses had been far from brotherly.

Chapter 6

Chloe Anne awoke late next morning after what had proved a deep sleep. As she sat up in bed, coming to a state of drowsy awareness, she stretched and yawned. Lord, but she had had the most incredible dream. It had been so vivid, so real. She had dreamed she had kissed Captain Trent under the mistletoe, touched his hand, and called him "Will."

But as her gaze roved about the nursery, she focused on the old-fashioned gown crumpled into a heap upon the floor, and memory of last night's escapade flooded back to her, her disastrous misadventure and its aftermath with Trent in the parlor.

Chloe felt her cheeks wash hot with confusion and was glad she was alone in the bedchamber. It had been no dream. She really had kissed the enemy. No, not the enemy, she was obliged to correct herself. She could scarce call the captain that any longer, not after the noble way he had spared her the humiliation of being discovered in her foolish masquerade, not after all the confidences they had shared before the fireside.

She was forced to acknowledge that Trent was not such a coldhearted man after all. For all his sternness, there was a gentleness about him, a gallantry very much like that of the knights of old.

Never would she forget the haunted look in his eyes as he had described the way Papa had died, the captain most bitterly blaming himself. For the first time since she had lost her father, Chloe had felt the need to give comfort rather than receive it, to soothe away the pain shadowing Trent's rugged features. In that instant, she had realized that hers had been the cold heart, set against Trent from the start.

If she had not feared that Emma was still so much in love with Mr. Henry, Chloe could have wished her sister joy of her engagement to the captain. He was indeed a fine man. But it was most strange. Her coming to know Will better, even to like him, only seemed to strengthen her opinion that his marriage to Emma would be very wrong.

Drawing up her knees beneath the coverlet, Chloe rested her head against them. Everything was so confusing. How much less complicated her life had been only a week ago, when she had been in blissful ignorance that Captain William Trent had been about to descend upon them. And yet she found she could no longer wish he had never come to Windhaven.

Oh no, she could not wish that at all.

He had brought with him the winds of change, whether for good or ill she was still not certain. She only knew that she felt more alive, more quickened with excitement than she had for a long time. It was almost like winter melting into spring. This morning she would not have been surprised to hear birds chirping among green leaves outside her window, to feel a flood of sunlight pouring into the room. But as she glanced up, she saw something that gave her far greater pleasure.

The windows were half frosted over with a crystalline substance that sparkled like diamonds. Beyond the glass, a few stray snowflakes danced through the air.

With a glad cry, Chloe flung back the coverlets and darted to the window, never minding the cold feel of the floorboards beneath her bare feet. She pressed her nose against the glass, shivering with delight.

After so many wretched, gray mornings of nothing but dampness and fog, it had snowed at last. The world was bright and new again. Not a deep snow, but enough to cover the gardens and the roof of the stables with a dusting of fairy white.

There was always something magical about the first snowfall. The bushes would be frosted like icy cakes, and the pond must be frozen over.

Unable to stand still, Chloe glanced eagerly about, longing for someone to share her pleasure. But Agnes had likely risen and crept out of their chamber long ago. And as if Agnes would have done anything more than look down her sharp little nose, declaring that the wonderland outside was but a natural consequence of the season, nothing to make such a pother about. Then she would dive back into some musty old book.

Chloe sighed, but she did not waste time repining over her lack of companionship. Instead, she stripped off her nightgown and hastened to get dressed. By the time she scrambled into a soft woolen gown the color of primroses, she felt the want of Agnes in a more practical manner. There was no one about to help her lace up the back of the gown.

Holding the material closed as best she could, Chloe crept cautiously down the hall to Lucy's room, certain of finding her in her chamber, still abed.

She was only half-right. Lucy was still in the room she shared with Emma, but surprisingly up and stirring. She stood before the dresser mirror, arranging an elegant shako upon her golden curls, the hat complementing the military cut of her new, blue velvet riding habit.

Chloe gaped in astonishment, but Lucy only laughed and spun her about to fasten up the back of the gown, all the while chattering gaily. "There you are, at last, Miss Slugabed. I told Emma someone ought to check on you, make certain you had not slipped into some trance, like that unfortunate princess Papa used to tell us about. You never even woke during all our excitement last night. What do you think? Captain Trent's steward was thrashing about in the throes of some horrid nightmare. It startled me so. I thought the house was being overrun by brigands."

Chloe felt a telltale blush rise into her cheeks, and she was glad she had her back to Lucy. As soon as Lucy had finished with the fastenings, Chloe peeked around, her gaze tracking from Lucy's riding habit to the riding gloves and fur-trimmed cape slung carelessly over a chair.

"Lucy," she said in accents of undisguised astonishment. "You are going out riding?"

"Mmm," Lucy said absently, taking one more peek in the mirror, adjusting her hat to a saucy angle.

"But didn't you notice? It snowed."

"Of course I noticed, you goose."

Chloe Anne was thoroughly nonplussed, knowing that Lucy was far more wont to curl up before the fire like a sleek cat on a day like this, rather than risk the frost nipping her nose to an unbecoming shade of red. Then a thought occurred to her.

"Oh!" she said. "Mr. Lathrop would not also happen to be going, would he?"

It was Lucy's turn to blush. She tossed her head in a manner of affected carelessness. "It so happens that he is. Charles—I mean, Mr. Lathrop—is quite mad about riding. I think he'd go out even if there were a blizzard. And someone must go with him to make certain he doesn't get lost again."

As though feeling the weight of Chloe's earnest stare, Lucy whipped about to glare at her. "And you needn't go thinking I am falling in love with the man."

"Why I . . . I d-didn't," Chloe stammered in protest. "I mean, I never—"

"Good! Because I am not. He is a very charming man and quite good-looking. But he is possessed of only a modest fortune and no title worth speaking of. I can do much better for myself in London."

"Perhaps you can, but—"

"I am glad we have that settled, then," Lucy said, jamming her fingers into her gloves. "Your romantic imaginings can be very tiresome sometimes, Chloe Anne."

Scooping up her cape, she swept majestically out of the room, leaving Chloe nigh incoherent with indignation and bewilderment. She was not quite sure what had just taken place, only that she had been most unjustly accused and Lucy was behaving very strangely.

But she was in far too sunny a mood to allow herself to be disconcerted for long. Slipping out of Lucy's room, Chloe headed downstairs, eager to discover what the rest of the household might be doing this morning.

The rest? She brought herself up short with an abashed half smile. She was honest enough to admit there was only one person whose whereabouts aroused her curiosity—that being a certain sea captain.

Belowstairs, she heard distinctly masculine voices coming from the region of the breakfast parlor. But before she could reach for the handle, the door swung open, and Mr. Doughty, on the point of charging out, nearly blundered into her.

"Oh, good morning, Miss Chloe," the sailor said with a respectful nod and his broad grin.

Her spirits somewhat subdued, she took a deep breath and greeted the steward, hastening on to frame her apology. "It was a beastly thing I did last night, giving you such a dreadful fright, and I am so very sorry."

Doughty, looking equally embarrassed, shuffled his feet. "Not at all, miss. 'Twas a capital jest. No need to look so down just for having a bit of fun. As for frightening me, pooh! I knew it was you all along." The burly seaman leaned forward in conspiratorial fashion. "Though I did think there was a moment there when you gave the captain quite a turn."

"You know, I believe there was." Chloe Anne pressed her hand to her lips to stifle a giggle, and Doughty chuckled heartily. As he stood aside to permit her to enter the breakfast parlor, she dimpled into a mischievous smile.

It was a smile she checked as she realized that Trent was already seated within and must have overheard this exchange. He quirked one brow in quizzical fashion.

"Of course, none of it was amusing at all," she said quickly. "And I'd never do it again."

Doughty agreed and beat a hasty retreat, closing the door behind him. Trent's lips twitched, but he rose respectfully at Chloe's entrance. She waved him back down.

"No, don't get up, Cap—Will. You mustn't let your breakfast get cold."

As she moved to help herself from the dishes assembled on the sideboard, Chloe could not help stealing a sidewise glance at him. He was clad in tight-fitting breeches and a dark blue frock coat that sported none of the glitter of his uniform. Yet he still presented a commanding presence, his dark hair swept back in flowing waves. He was handsome enough to make any maid's heart pound a little harder. Perhaps Emma truly was reconciled to the prospect of marrying him. Chloe Anne knew that if the choice had been hers . . .

Blushing, she checked her thoughts, which were both wayward and improper. Lowering her gaze, she fixed her attention upon securing herself a bit of toast and a cup of tea. She managed to compose herself by the time she returned to the table, although she shyly ducked her head when Will held her chair for her. It would have astonished her to learn that he was also feeling the absence of his usual composure. He found it difficult to admit how eagerly he had been awaiting her appearance. He had spent a restless night, deeply troubled by the feelings she had aroused in him with that innocent kiss under the mistletoe. But he had managed to convince himself it was all right. She was going to become his sister, and it was the proper thing to entertain some fondness for her.

Indeed, it would have been impossible not to be fond of Chloe Anne. Trent had never seen anything so charming as the way she had apologized to Mr.

Doughty. Her soft, honey-colored curls framing that delicate face, those wide blue eyes so contrite. With such a look, a man could forgive her anything, Trent thought, even to sinking his ship to the bottom of the Channel. England had plenty of boats; there was only one Chloe Anne.

Astonished by the foolish notions flitting through his brain, Trent concentrated upon his plate, which was heaping with eggs and a large grilled beefsteak.

He ate with gusto until he became aware that Chloe was staring at him. Flushing a little, he lowered his fork.

"You'll have to excuse me if I seem a perfect glutton," he said. "After so long at sea, when breakfast is often a hard biscuit alive with weevils, something like this seems like pure ambrosia."

"Oh, no. Don't apologize," Chloe said, moving to refill his coffee cup. "I didn't mean to stare. It was only so pleasant for once to see you really enjoying something."

"Do I really seem that much of a dull old stick?"

"No, only surpassingly serious. I would wager you have already forgotten you are supposed to be on holiday and have arranged some sort of grim schedule for today."

"Naturally, I had planned to meet with Mr. Martin, and then there are some accounts to be gone over—" Trent broke off with a guilty laugh. "And what plans have you formed for your day, ma'am?"

"Me?" Chloe Anne leaned against the back of her chair, her eyes becoming dreamy. "I intend to do something of great importance. I am going outside to make footprints in the snow, and then if I can bully Agnes into going with me, I shall go skating on the pond."

"I fear you have little chance of that, my dear. I believe Agnes has already barricaded herself in the library with a most ponderous-looking tome."

"And Lucy and Mr. Lathrop have gone riding." Chloe gave a most disconsolate sigh. "And Emma never skates."

"In any case, Emma is already engaged in interviewing prospective housemaids by my insistence. I looked at your sister's hands and was appalled to see how chapped her fingers are becoming from all her work in the kitchens."

Chloe Anne only nodded. An image rose in her mind of Trent examining Emma's hands, and she could fancy how tenderly he must have done so. The thought produced a curious and wistful ache in her heart.

She was rather glad of the diversion provided by Polly and Old Meg entering the breakfast parlor. Chloe reached eagerly for the small purse she had brought with her. It was Boxing Day, a time customarily set aside for rewarding the service of one's family retainers, and none deserved it more than these loyal and faithful friends.

But as she started to spill into her hand the bright shillings she had so carefully saved, the elderly cook and pert housemaid were already making their curtsies to the captain.

"Begging your pardon, Captain." Old Meg beamed. "We didn't wish to intrude upon your breakfast, but Polly and me could wait no longer to thank you for your generous gift."

"Truly," Polly gushed. "I never had five pounds all at once in me life before."

Five pounds? Chloe felt her own smile waver. The hoard of shillings clutched in her fist seemed pathetic by comparison, and she whisked them under the table.

Trent looked exceedingly uncomfortable to be the recipient of so much gratitude. He accepted all the thanks in his usual stern fashion. When the two women had gone, he turned to regard Chloe Anne. She feared some of her chagrin must have showed in her face, for he asked anxiously, "Did I do something wrong? I heard Emma speaking of Boxing Day this morning, and I thought it was the proper thing to do—"

"Oh yes, very proper," Chloe said, attempting to surreptitiously stuff the shillings back into her purse. But to her horror, a few escaped to roll across the table and settle near Trent's coffee cup.

As he returned them to her, she saw his eyes light with comprehension.

"You should have gone ahead and made your gift, Chloe Anne," he said.

Chloe affected a shrug. "What would shillings be compared to pounds?"

"A great deal more when given out of love instead of duty."

His perception both touched and astonished her. "I thought you didn't believe in love," she could not help reminding him with a tiny smile.

"I don't recall ever saying that, ma'am." Despite his gruff tone, he smiled back at her.

On an impulse, she reached across the table, covering his hand with her own. "Oh, Will, forget about your stuffy meeting with Mr. Martin. Come skating with me instead."

He laughed. "I have never been on skates in my life, Chloe Anne."

"That doesn't matter. I am sure you could learn easily. After all, you must be very agile, the way you sailors go climbing about among all that rigging."

"It has been a good many years since I have been obliged to do anything like that, my dear. A captain only has to stroll about the deck, getting fat and lazy while he bellows out orders."

Chloe ran a skeptical and admiring gaze over Trent's lean, muscular frame. "I can't imagine you ever strolling. The bellowing, however—"

Trent cut her off firmly. "Besides, I have no skates."

"Papa's are still about somewhere. I am sure they would fit you."

Although Trent continued to shake his head and laugh at her mad proposal, Chloe detected a certain wistfulness in his eyes. She did not know why she continued to press him. Perhaps it was because she was haunted by the image of a lonely young boy who had spent far too many of his holidays standing to attention aboard the deck of a ship.

Squeezing his hand, she peered up at him through the thickness of her lashes.

"Oh, please," she said.

"You only want to see me make a great fool of myself," he grumbled, but Chloe sensed him weakening.

"Very well," he said. "But you must promise not to laugh at me."

Chloe, concealing a grin of triumph, gave him her most solemn promise.

The pond that stood just beyond the stables at Windhaven normally played host to a brood of fat, white ducks and a badger family that crept out of the woods to drink. But winter had finally rendered the water into a sheet of ice as smooth as a lady's looking glass.

Bundled up in her best green coat, Chloe glided along, the wind whipping beneath her bonnet and stinging her cheeks a bright pink. She whirled happily about in a circle before turning to check the captain's progress.

Trent smothered an oath as his feet flew out from under him for the third time. He slid across the frozen surface on the back of his heavy frieze jacket. Chloe brought her gloved hands up to her mouth to stifle her merriment.

Sprawled at her feet, Trent glowered up at her. "You gave me your oath, madam."

"Aye, I . . . I did, and I am not l-laughing." Chloe gasped on a chuckle. Balancing firmly on the blades of her own skates, she extended one hand to help him up. " 'Tis only you do l-look a trifle undignified. I cannot help imagining what your friend Mr. Lathrop might say."

"At your peril, you breathe a word of this to him or anyone else," Trent said with a mock growl. He regained his footing but still appeared most unsteady. As he cautiously moved one skate forward, Chloe clung to his arm, trying to help by giving him a small push.

She panted a little at the exertion of helping to balance Trent's large frame. "Now I know what you captains must go through when you try to launch a ship."

After another tentative glide, Trent started slipping again, but this time, as he went down, he clung to Chloe Anne, taking her with him.

He landed on his back once more, his arms banding about Chloe, causing her to fall on top of him. With a soft gasp, she raised up a little, trying to shake the hair from her eyes. "You did that on purpose," she said.

Trent's mouth curved into a mischief-laden smile. "A good captain always goes down with her ship, my dear."

Chloe tried to be indignant but failed, dimpling at him instead. Her face was so close to his, she could actually feel the warmth of his breath against her cheek. She became aware of other things as well, the frieze jacket that seemed to carry with it the salt tang of the sea, the liquid silver of his eyes, the solid feel of his body beneath her.

A tingling sensation worked through her veins. Feeling shy and confused, Chloe made haste to scramble out of his arms. Trent struggled to a sitting position.

"A good captain also knows when to strike his colors," he said. Bending one leg forward, he began to undo the strap of his skate.

"You cannot give up that easily," Chloe cried. "Is this the spirit that won Trafalgar?"

He shot her a disgruntled look, but by dint of much coaxing she got him back on his feet. Trent suddenly thought of a dozen reasons why they should return to the house, a hundred pressing matters requiring his attention, but Chloe refuted them all.

It took the better part of the morning and several more tumbles before he learned to maintain his balance. But Trent was possessed of a natural athletic grace, and although he grumbled that "this was worse than acquiring one's sea legs," he was soon keeping pace with Chloe Anne, threatening to have her clapped in irons if she attempted to twirl him in a circle.

They linked arms, skating in companionable silence, round and round the pond, blowing out breathy clouds of steam as they glided forward in perfect rhythm. The snow-trimmed pines, the hedgerows, and the frost-capped stables passed by in a blur of white.

"Are you getting cold?" Trent asked, tucking her arm more snugly beneath his, pressing her hand within his own.

"No, not a bit of it." Chloe tipped her face up to the cloudy, gray sky, feeling as warm as though she were basking in a flood of sunlight. "It's a glorious day. I haven't felt this happy since . . . since I can scarce remember."

"Aye," Trent agreed quietly. He was not given to such rushes of feeling, but he knew what she meant. He was filled with a sense of contentment as sweet as it was rare.

"You are skating very well now," she said. "Are you not glad I persuaded you to try it?"

"It's pleasant enough when one remains upright, rather like sailing before a good strong wind."

Chloe fell silent a moment, then astonished him by asking suddenly, "What is it like, Will, being aboard your ship all the time?"

"Well, *Gloriana* is a ship of the line with three decks and eighty-seven cannon—"

"I don't mean that," she said with one of her delightful trills of laughter. "Tell me what it *feels* like."

Trent rolled his eyes. Chloe Anne had a habit of asking a man the most confounded things. If any other lady had posed him such a fool question, he would have found some curt but polite way to dismiss it. But for Chloe, he caught himself struggling to oblige her with an answer.

"Well, at times life at sea can be hard, sometimes even monotonous, but there is always . . ." His voice trailed away as he began to consider sights and sounds he had always taken for granted, but he achieved a kind of wonder as he tried to describe them for Chloe Anne. How fresh the wind blew out at sea, how it sang through the rigging, how diamond-hard and bright the stars appeared on a clear night, the way the salt spray could sting one's cheeks. He spoke of how humble a man often felt surrounded by nothing but sea and sky, how frightened when the waves turned black and pounded against the side of the ship, the deck heaving beneath one's feet, how exhilarating that feeling of riding out a storm, besting it.

"It all sounds prodigiously exciting," Chloe Anne said. She peeked up at him from beneath the brim of her bonnet and added hesitantly, "But I fear Mr. Doughty doesn't like sailing as well as you do. He told me how he came to be on your ship. He didn't want to be impressed into the navy."

"Few men do," Trent said wryly, a little amused to hear the burly seaman had made Chloe Anne his confidante. "Would Mr. Doughty have preferred being hanged for smuggling?"

"No. He is grateful his life was spared. But he misses his home and his poor gray-haired old mum."

Trent had to choke back a laugh, for Chloe looked so mournfully serious. The phrase about the "old mum" had to have been Doughty's own, echoed unconsciously by Chloe Anne. The old rascal certainly had been pitching it rum to the girl.

"I fear what Doughty misses most is his old free-booting way of life," Trent said. "A little naval discipline will do him no harm."

"But to be forced to serve for so many years! That seems rather harsh for just smuggling a very tiny drop of brandy."

"Aye, just a drop or two. Only five hundred kegs."

"I don't care. I think he has been punished enough. If he hates being in the navy and wants to go home—"

"Chloe Anne," Trent interrupted. He halted their progress around the pond long enough to direct an intensely serious look at her. "It is kind of you to take an interest in Mr. Doughty's welfare, but you shouldn't encourage him to lament his lot. He might become tempted to do something that he shouldn't. Desertion is a serious crime."

"Yes, but—"

Trent laid his fingers gently against her lips to silence her. "You must allow that I know best in matters regarding my own crew. Your meddling in Doughty's affairs could only bring disaster, Chloe Anne. One should never attempt to interfere in someone else's life."

"You mean like I tried to do with you and Emma?"

"Well . . . well, yes."

She pulled a face, then sighed. "Perhaps you are right. I shall try to make a greater effort not to be so . . . so *busy*." But even as she made this vow, she looked far from convinced. She lapsed into silence, and they resumed skating. Trent half feared that his rebuke, even gentle as it was, might have destroyed the newfound harmony between them.

But Chloe quickly recovered from any chagrin she might have felt and once more began to pelt him with questions about life in the navy. She wanted to hear about some of his own exploits, his ambitions, even his dreams.

Trent could not remember ever having been persuaded to talk so much about himself before, especially to a lady. If Chloe's interest had appeared at all coy or feigned, he would have stopped at once, feeling like the greatest fool.

But she halted in front of him, catching up both his hands in her eagerness to hear more, her eyes alight as she drank in every word. He found himself confessing to thoughts and aspirations that would have caused his grandfather, the old admiral, to roll in his watery grave.

". . . And after working so hard to make a ship seaworthy, training your crew to perform all the maneuvers to perfection until you and they are almost at one with the ship, it seems the most damnable folly, the most senseless waste, merely to become the target for cannon fire. When this blasted war is over, it has always been my dream to have done with the navy and . . ."

"And?" Chloe urged when he hesitated.

"And to outfit my own ship, a three-masted frigate, perhaps with a handpicked crew, to sail all the way around the world, to have the leisure to really explore some of those faraway places like the West Indies or Barbados."

"Jamaica?" Chloe breathed.

"Perhaps even the Orient."

"Oh," she lamented. "Why is it that men get to do all the exciting things and have all the adventures?"

Trent laughed. "I have heard of some merchant captains who take their ladies with them and adorn their cabins with all the comforts of home."

"Oh, Will. That would be wonderful. I—" The sparkle in Chloe's eyes dimmed. "I don't suppose Emma would much care for that."

"No," Trent said slowly, "I don't suppose that she would."

Chloe Anne suddenly felt very self-conscious. She carefully disengaged her hands from Trent's grasp.

"It must be very hard to be a sailor's wife," she said, "when your husband is gone so much of the time at sea."

"I assure you that Emma will always be well cared for—" Trent began hastily.

"I don't doubt that she will. I never supposed it would be as difficult for her as it is for Sukey Green, and yet—" Chloe swallowed. She had told Trent she would stop meddling, but it was a promise she was finding difficult to keep. "As hard as it has been for Sukey, she once told me of the one thought that sustains her. No matter how far away her Tom might be, his heart is always left with her."

Trent gave her a taut smile. "I did not know it was possible for a man to be so discriminating with his anatomy."

Chloe suppressed a sigh, realizing that Trent did not understand at all what she was trying to tell him: that no matter how many comforts he might leave Emma surrounded by, she was always going to be bereft of one thing—a husband's love.

The wind that whistled across the pond seemed to have gotten more brisk, and Chloe shivered. When Trent suggested it was time to go back to the house, she made no protest. The glow that had surrounded their golden morning spent together seemed to have vanished as rapidly as if the gray clouds overhead had blotted out the sun.

Chloe Ann felt peculiarly loath to discuss her outing with the captain to anyone. Later, when she encountered Emma in the parlor, Chloe started when her older sister brought up the subject.

Emma looked up from her mending with a serene smile. "Ah, so there you are. You and Trent were gone so long, I feared the pair of you had run off together."

"Oh, n-no," Chloe stammered, horrified to feel her face turn a bright red. "I only took Will—that is, I was only teaching him to skate."

"And I was only teasing you, dearest." Emma laughed. "Of course I knew that you were down at the pond. So you and the captain have managed to become friends at last. I am very happy."

Chloe could not help regarding her sister earnestly. "Are you, Emma? Truly happy, that is."

Emma's gaze dropped back to the needlework in her lap. "Certainly, I am most content."

Chloe did not find this reply reassuring. Happy and content were far from being the same thing. Would it do any good to broach the subject of Mr. Henry again? Apparently not, for as though she feared Chloe might be about to say something more, Emma was already folding her mending back into her workbasket, declaring she had best see how Old Meg was coming with the things for tea.

Rushing out, Emma paused on the threshold to say, "Thank you again, Chloe Anne, for making such an effort to be cordial to Captain Trent, to keep him occupied this morning. I really am most grateful to you."

And the melancholy thing was, Chloe thought, that it was perfectly true. Emma's eyes did shine with a real gratitude. A gratitude that left Chloe feeling sad and even more strange—a little guilty.

Chapter 7

The days seemed to be slipping away faster than the tide raking sand from the shore. Settled behind the desk in Windhaven's small, musty library, Trent thumbed through the personal log that he always kept with him. As he dipped his pen into the inkwell, he was startled to note what the date should be: December 31, the last day of 1807.

He could hardly credit it. He had been here at Windhaven an entire sennight, yet it felt as if he had just arrived. Never before had he experienced such a swift passage of time, especially not while on leave from his ship. Indeed, after one week, time usually seemed to grind to a halt, with him chafing against the hours, longing to return to sea.

Still disbelieving, he turned back one page to recheck that he had not made some error. No, today was indeed New Year's Eve. That meant only five more days remained until Twelfth Night, five more sunsets until he was a married man and on his way back to his ship. The thought was almost alarming. It was as if he rode the crest of some tidal wave, his destiny quite out of his control. He attempted to dismiss the odd feeling, telling himself he was merely disturbed because so many days had sped by and he had accomplished very little.

Somehow he had never met with Mr. Martin to

go over the accounts. Nor had he ever succeeded in making a thorough-enough inspection of the house. He had also neglected to take a riding tour of the estate and meet his new tenants.

Then what the deuce had he done with all of his time? He began flipping through all the recent entries in his diary. As he skimmed the pages, his mouth curved into a rueful half smile.

December 26—Boxing Day—went ice skating with Chloe Anne. Left hip sadly bruised. Took a most welcome hot bath.

December 27—Feast of the Innocents. Escorted Chloe into village. Called at cottage of that little girl Peggety, who speaks such an extraordinary language. Chloe brought a posset to the mother. Mrs. Green appears as interesting as ever and mighty uncomfortable.

December 28—Chloe showed me the local cliffs and beach. She wanted to learn how to dance a sailor's jig to the hornpipe. Astonished to discover that after all these years, I still know how to do so.

December 29—Helped Chloe Anne hitch the farm horse to the sleigh. Obliged to drive out with her lest she upset this ancient vehicle into a ditch. She didn't. I did. Luckily the bank where I overturned us had a reasonably soft padding of snow. Fear that Lathrop will never let me hear the end of it.

December 30—Bitter-cold day. Stayed indoors as my throat was feeling a bit raw. Chloe insisted upon trying to make me a blancmange. I went to the kitchens to assist her. The pair of us created such a disaster Old Meg threatened to give in her notice. Emma only laughed.

As Trent perused this last entry, it disturbed him to note how infrequently Emma's name appeared. Even without that hard evidence, he was obliged to admit that he had been neglecting his intended bride. Not that he was entirely to blame for that. When any outing was proposed, Emma always had some domestic matter that claimed her attention—and this besides the fact that two stout wenches from the village had been recently engaged into service at Windhaven.

Emma had been quite willing to send him off with her younger sister, and Chloe Anne, with her exuberant pastimes, was far too innocently beguiling. But Trent saw that it was a poor if not improper state of affairs. He should have made some effort to become better acquainted with his future wife. That he had not done so was a grave dereliction of duty.

With only five days until the wedding, the situation required immediate remedy. With this view in mind, Trent closed up his log and summoning Polly, the maid, dispatched a request to Emma that she join him in the parlor that afternoon, affording him a little time alone in her company.

Request? Nay, he feared he had framed it more like a command, as though he were summoning his first mate to wait upon him in his cabin. But Emma did not seem to mind, for she sent back a polite acceptance.

Chloe Anne would have teased him, given him a far more difficult time. When he became too highhanded, she was still inclined to snap him off a roguish salute, her blue eyes sparkling, that mischievous dimple. . . .

Trent sucked in his breath, striving to banish the image. He thought entirely too much about Chloe Anne of late. It simply wouldn't do.

At precisely a quarter to three, he entered the parlor, as stiff and formal as though he had come courting a young lady whose hand he had yet to win. Emma greeted him in equally grave fashion.

They took up their positions opposite each other, she seated upon the wing-back chair, Trent settling upon the settee. He smiled at her. She smiled back. Never, Trent thought wryly, had two people been more cheerfully determined to be obliging to each other.

After the first attempts at conversation, Emma seemed unable to refrain from diving into her workbasket. She pulled forth a red wool sock she had been knitting and set to work on it. His bride was obviously a lady of great industry, never one to let her hands remain idle. It was an admirable trait and one he should have greatly approved. Why, then, did the incessant click of those knitting needles grate upon his nerves?

He was not one given to indulging in unnecessary movements, but he caught himself tapping his fingers against his knee. They talked of the weather, the indifferent harvest, and the shocking price of candles. What the deuce they were going to discuss next was more than he knew. He deferred to Emma, but she flung the choice right back at him.

"You may discourse upon anything you like," she said amiably. "I am a great listener."

Which left him precisely nowhere, for he was not a great talker. There was no question of regaling Emma with any of the sea tales Chloe Anne always badgered him for. He had a lowering notion that Emma would only politely remark, "How interesting," and then he would feel like a complete dolt.

At last, in desperation, he said, "I procured a special license for our marriage. Did I tell you that?"

Emma merely nodded, and he winced. Yes, by thunder, he had told her that, several times, at least.

He continued, "I hope you are not too disappointed that our wedding will not be a grander affair."

"Not at all. A simple wedding was all I ever desired. No more than my family to be present and then a small breakfast to be served after the ceremony."

Trent cleared his throat. It was a ticklish subject, but he felt he had to broach it. "And it is all right with you that Mr. Henry should perform the ceremony?"

There was a slight pause in Emma's movements, and then the needles clicked more furiously than ever. "Certainly. He is the local vicar. Who else should perform the service?"

It was a most sensible reply, but Trent was conscious of a feeling of disappointment. He was dismayed to realize he had almost hoped to hear her say it was not all right for Mr. Henry to officiate, perhaps even not all right for there to be a wedding at all.

Trent drew himself upright, forcing his own fingers to be still. What was wrong with him to be thinking such a thing? Likely only nerves, a last-minute panic that any long-term bachelor must feel when finally confronting the altar.

After another lengthy silence, Emma inquired, "Have you reached any decision about where we shall live? I know Chloe finally took you over the old part of Windhaven. I daresay you found it in sad case."

Trent agreed, although he feared he had not noticed as much as he should have. He had spent his entire inspection lingering with Chloe in what had been the west wing's ballroom, listening to her conjure up visions of dashing cavaliers and lovely ladies moving through the steps of some lively dance until he had been almost able to see the plumed hats and the panniered gowns reflected in the hall's cracked mirrors.

"Actually," he was astonished to hear himself saying, "I have been giving some thought to renovating Windhaven."

Emma frowned a little. "Is that practical? I fear it would be shockingly expensive, and I thought you wanted—" She stopped short, blushing. "Oh, forgive me. I didn't mean . . . Of course, the decision is yours alone."

"Indeed, it is not. Sometimes, Emma, I wish you will remember that you are going to be my wife, not merely my housekeeper." He had not meant to sound so sharp, and when Emma flinched, he strove to gentle his voice. "I value your opinion, my dear. Would you prefer to live closer to London as I once suggested?"

"It would be pleasant to be nearer to Cousin Harriet," Emma conceded. "Lucy could be presented, which is something she has wanted forever. And Chloe, too, is of an age when she should be meeting some eligible young men."

"So she is," Trent said. He jerked abruptly to his feet, suddenly finding this tête-à-tête with Emma far from satisfactory. Yet she was being everything a man could desire, sweet, quiet, deferring to his every word. Was there such a thing as a woman being too obliging?

Feeling strangely irritable, he stalked to the window and stared moodily past the curtain. Emma continued to knit, allowing the conversation to fade to nothing. But Trent did not find it a companionable silence. Rather, it engendered in him a restless feeling similar to those endless, nerve-grinding days when his ship had stood becalmed, waiting, praying for even one small breath of wind.

Catching a blur of movement beyond the panes, Trent edged the curtain further aside. It had snowed again last night, covering the ground with a fresh layering of white. Lucy, Lathrop, and Chloe Anne were romping through the garden like children.

Even through the glass, Trent could catch the faint echoes of laughter, Lathrop's dismayed protest as the two ladies outflanked him, pelting him mercilessly with snowballs. When he scooped up a handful of snow himself to retaliate, Chloe and Lucy fled, shrieking.

Trent did not know what caused Chloe to suddenly glance back toward the house. It was almost as if she sensed him standing by the window. Her green coat dusted with snow, her rosy, flushed features framed by the large poke-front bonnet, she darted in a little closer, like some graceful snow maiden.

Gleefully, she bent down to scoop up another handful of snow. Her dimples quivering with mischief, she flung it at the window. Although protected by the glass, Trent started back involuntarily at the sudden shower of white. She wrinkled her pert nose at him, pulling the most saucy face before she turned and raced back to the garden.

The urge to fling open the casement, climb out, and offer pursuit was strong. He could imagine so clearly overtaking her, spinning her around in his arms until the winter air echoed with her bright laughter. Trent caught himself reaching for the sash. He stayed his hand, both puzzled and disturbed by the yearning that flooded through him.

Perhaps it would be better when he returned to his ship. He was becoming as giddy as a schoolboy, forever wanting the world to be all holiday as it was near Chloe Anne. Responsibility and duty were two words he had nigh forgotten this Christmastide.

He forced himself to forget about joining Chloe Anne in the garden, instead returning to resume his position on the settee. He spent the rest of the afternoon stoically thinking up new topics for conversation and watching Emma's needles go click, click, click.

Lathrop had gone off to the stables for his daily ride. Lucy did not seem disposed to accompany him, much to Chloe Anne's dismay. These past few days she had come to dread being left alone with Lucy, hearing her confidences.

Chloe's beautiful older sister could seem to talk about nothing but love, or rather her lack of it, insisting over and over again that she stood in no danger of losing her heart to Charles Lathrop.

After their walk in the gardens, Chloe made haste toward the servant's entryway to shed her wet boots by the kitchen fire. She had hoped to outstrip Lucy, but Lucy ran to catch up with her.

When Chloe heard her sister draw breath to launch into speech, Chloe forestalled her with an imploring gesture. "Oh, please, Lucy. I really do not think I can bear to hear again how much you are not in love with Mr. Lathrop."

Lucy's rosebud-shaped mouth drew down into a

157

pout. "I wasn't going to say anything of the kind. Really, Chloe Anne. You have been cross as crabs of late. I don't know what is the matter with you." After a pause she added mournfully, "Nor me either."

When Chloe refused to venture any suggestions, Lucy bridled defensively. "I know it is imprudent to spend so much time in Charles's company, but I cannot seem to help myself. I always want to be with him. When he is gone, I catch myself listening for his footfall on the stairs. I spend all my time daydreaming, thinking of what I'll say to him when next we meet, all the little things I cannot wait to share." She groaned. "Am I quite mad, Chloe Anne?"

Chloe could only shrug helplessly. If Lucy was indeed insane, Chloe feared that her own mind was similarly afflicted. Lucy's description of her behavior toward Mr. Lathrop too nearly matched Chloe's experience with regard to Will Trent.

She and Lucy trudged through the snow in silence. But just as they arrived at the kitchen door, Lucy pulled up short with a faint sigh of despair. "Oh, it's no good pretending any longer. I know what has happened to me." Lucy stamped her foot, her cornflower blue eyes blinking back furious tears. "Despite all my best efforts, I have gone and fallen in love with that wretched man."

Love? Could that possibly be what was tormenting poor Lucy? If that were so, then what about Chloe Anne, whose symptoms were so much the same? No, that was utter nonsense. She could not possibly be falling in love with the man intended to be Emma's husband. Chloe shrank from the very notion, finding it too dreadful to contemplate.

"Oh, Lucy," she quavered. "Do you really think . . .

I mean, all that you have been saying . . . Is that what being in love is like? Are you sure?"

"As sure as anyone can ever be of such a thing. What is more, I believe Charles also cares for me. There have been several times when I feared him to be on the verge of speaking, but I have always stopped him."

Lucy thrust her hands more deeply into her muff and frowned. "What a dreadful coil!"

Yet even as she said this, her lips trembling, Lucy's expression became softer, more tender than Chloe Anne had ever seen her look before. She mused, "Though I suppose it would not be so bad, marrying Charles. I never truly wanted to wed an earl. Being called 'my lady' all the time would become dreadfully tedious.

"Of course, Charles and I think differently. I would want to go to London for the Season, and he wouldn't. We'd have dreadful rows, but always in the end he would take me in his arms and . . ." Lucy heaved a rapturous sigh. "It would be quite divine."

Whirling suddenly, she enveloped Chloe Anne in an impulsive hug. "Oh, thank you, Chloe Anne. I am so glad we had this little talk. It has made everything so wonderfully clear."

Before Chloe could recover her wits, Lucy darted ahead of her into the house. But Chloe remained frozen on the doorstep, unable to curb a fluttering of resentment. Maybe everything was now crystal-clear to Lucy, but certainly not to Chloe Anne.

Still, if Lucy had fallen in love with Mr. Lathrop, if he returned her regard, Chloe would certainly rejoice for both of them. It would be a grand thing for Lucy, far more likely to bring her happiness than any of her more worldly schemes. Mr. Lathrop was such a good-natured young man, charming and very eligible.

Now, Will Trent, on the other hand, was not in the least eligible. He was already betrothed to her oldest sister. It didn't matter that theirs would be a marriage of convenience, not affection, that Emma by rights should have been marrying someone else. The fact remained that the wedding would take place in five days, and for Chloe to be harboring any notions about Trent was downright ... *treasonous.*

It was absurd for Chloe Anne to even imagine falling in love with him. Had she not disliked him amazingly upon their first acquaintance? But that all seemed such a long time ago, another lifetime, practically. Days had intervened since then, days when she seemed to be with him every waking moment until she knew almost everything about him, all his dreams, all his fears, how generous he could be, how caring, despite his gruff exterior. She even knew his flaws, and he *did* have them, she reminded herself fiercely.

He could be so unbelievably obstinate, especially when he was convinced he was right. Sometimes he was so stuffed with common sense that he could not see beyond the end of his own nose.

But it was such a handsome nose, carved on the same strong lines as the rest of his face. And his eyes—they were what Chloe had come to think of as a deep-sea gray. She loved how they lightened those rare times when Will realized even a captain was permitted to laugh.

Resting one arm along the stonework of the house, Chloe buried her forehead against it, appalled by the direction of her thoughts but totally powerless to check them. This was all Lucy's fault, forever rattling on about being in love. It was as catching as a contagious disease.

But she was being most unfair to blame Lucy. Even if Lucy had never breathed a word of her own romance, Chloe knew the realization would have overtaken her eventually. She had simply been fighting it, but to no avail.

She had fallen in love with Will Trent.

There—she had admitted it, if not aloud, then most certainly to herself. Chloe held her breath, waiting. She had always imagined that the day she acknowledged such a thing, there would be birds singing, rainbows in the sky, riotous springtime even in the midst of winter. But there was nothing but this horrid burning ache in her chest just as though she had been shot through the heart.

It was so disloyal to Emma, but Chloe could not help pondering how different things might have been. If Emma and Mr. Henry had only set aside their scruples and eloped. Then when Will had come to Windhaven to do his duty, he would have had to select another sister. Perhaps then . . .

Chloe swallowed hard. No, he would have likely picked Lucy or even Agnes, both more sensible creatures than she. Chloe knew she amused Trent sometimes, but never would he have wanted to wed the sister whose head was oft so far in the clouds, she tripped over her own two feet.

Tears stung her eyes, and she dashed them aside. The old longing for her father came back to her, strong and fierce. Never had she stood in such need of his comfort and advice. She could almost picture the sage way he would have shaken his gray head, how gently he would have patted her cheek. What was it he had once said to her?

Hearts can be broken, Chloe Anne. But they do

mend, and oftentimes one is a little wiser for the wear.

She didn't feel any wiser at the moment, only completely wretched. But she realized she could not spend the rest of her life moping by the kitchen door. One of the new housemaids had come out and already leveled her a very odd stare.

Her shoulders drooping, Chloe made her way into the kitchen. Something warm and fragrant was bubbling in a huge kettle over the fire, but Chloe had never had less of an appetite.

Mr. Doughty appeared in far different case. Hovering near the larder, he was scooping up an entire loaf of bread. Or so Chloe thought at first, then concluded she must be mistaken. Why on earth would Mr. Doughty shove a loaf of bread inside a canvas sack?

Whatever he was doing, he had his back to her and seemed far too absorbed to pay her any heed. Chloe heaved a deep sigh as she plunked down on a three-legged stool to pull off her boots. Mr. Doughty whipped around with a loud oath.

"Oh, Miss Chloe!"

"Sorry," she said, forcing a smile. "I didn't mean to frighten you."

"You didn't. That is, I . . . I was just so intent on polishin' up the cap'n's boots, I fear I didn't notice ye come in."

That seemed an odd thing for Doughty to say. Will's high-top boots, looking much the worse for a layering of mud, stood perched upon the hearth untouched.

Doughty added with a sheepish grin, "I mean, I was just lookin' about for some champagne. I heard tell it does wonders when added to the blackin'."

"Well, you won't find any here. It has been a long

time since we have seen any champagne at Windhaven."

"Suppose I'll just have to make do without it." Doughty rubbed his hands together in hearty fashion. "The cap'n's boots took quite a beatin' on yer last walk, Miss Chloe. He'll have my hide if I don't do something to salvage 'em."

As he strode to the hearth to begin, Chloe rose hastily, fearing the big seaman might want to engage her in one of their long, cozy chats. She was in no mood for conversation with anyone. But her fears were for naught. Doughty appeared just as somber as she. He commenced his task of polishing with a grim set to his lips, for once even forgetting to whistle.

Chloe slipped past him and had nearly reached the door when she heard him call, "Miss Chloe?"

Glancing back, she saw Doughty bending over the boots, the exertion making him red in the face. He muttered, "After supper tonight, ma'am, I'd be obliged if ye had a word with the cap'n for me. Tell him . . . tell him I said that I was real sorry."

"Of course," Chloe agreed with a slight frown. How strange that Doughty should want her to convey his apologies or that he should imagine that Will would be in any kind of fret. Even if the boots were ruined, they were only his second-best pair. Yet she was too consumed with her own misery to puzzle over Doughty's words for long. By the time she left the kitchen, the odd conversation went right out of her head.

She was more worried about how she was ever going to face Will again. She feared he might read her folly in her eyes. She had never been good at the arts of concealment. If only she could somehow hide away in her room until it was time for Will to go back to his ship. A ridiculous notion, for there were five more days and the wedding itself to contend with.

For once, she simply must learn how to dissemble. Most of all, she had to avoid being alone with Will, to hold him at a distance. But it was one thing to form such a resolution, quite another to carry it out.

Chloe did not find it natural to turn a cold shoulder, to withhold her smiles from anyone that she loved. And she was rapidly discovering she had never loved anyone more than she did Will Trent.

She managed to scrape through supper by sitting at the opposite end of the table from him. But the evening ahead presented a far greater challenge, even more so because it was New Year's Eve. It was the one night of the year they kept late hours at Windhaven, stayed up to watch the old year fade, to welcome in the new.

When the gentlemen joined the ladies in the parlor, Will tried to approach Chloe on several occasions, but she was quick to skitter away. She conceived the happy notion of entertaining the others with a magic lantern show. At least in the semidarkness, she might better conceal her feelings.

Agnes retired promptly, declaring herself too old for such childish entertainments. But the rest gathered round while Chloe brought forth the box of color transparencies and subjected them to an endless display of scenes upon the parlor wall.

The magic lantern always used to delight Chloe as a child, those light images of monarchs and maidens, knights and dragons, even a terrifying specter or two.

But tonight the scenes flashed before her in a dull

blur, her hands moving almost mechanically to slide one transparency out, put another one in.

At some point after much whispering and giggling, Lucy and Lathrop escaped from the parlor. Chloe hardly noticed at first, only gradually becoming aware of the silence. Daring a glance behind her, she could make out Emma's form. Exhausted after a day of instructing the new laundry maid in her duties, Emma had slumped down on the settee, fast asleep. As for Trent, he, too, appeared to have vanished.

Chloe knew she should have been relieved at his absence, not continuing to look about for him with a wistful ache in her heart. Then she felt a light touch upon her hand. She jumped, realizing that Trent had stalked silently up beside her. He stood, his looming muscular frame lost in shadow, the angular lines of his profile cast into sharp relief by the lantern's glow.

"That is an enchanting castle, Chloe Anne," he said. "But I believe you have already shown it thrice."

"Have I? I-I am sorry." Chloe hastened to change the transparency. He checked her movement, his fingers gently but firmly banding about her wrist.

"Chloe Anne, have I done something wrong?"

No, she wanted to cry. Unfortunately, he had done everything right, right enough to make her want to cast herself into his arms forever. She squirmed to free her hand, fearing he would feel the way her pulse thundered beneath his touch.

"Nothing is wrong," she managed to say. "Why do you ask?"

"You are so quiet tonight, and I feel as if you are avoiding me. Did I offend you earlier when I suggested the decorations come down? That was only because when I touched up against the mantel, I came away with a handful of pine needles."

"No, I am not angry about that. I daresay you had forgotten what I said about the bad luck."

"Yes, ill fortune betide us if the holly is removed before Twelfth Night, and I would not wish for any more bad luck. Somehow I feel like the most misfortunate fellow alive because you have not smiled at me all evening."

She tried to force a smile, a casual friendly one, but found she couldn't. She busied herself changing the transparency even though she had lost her audience. Striving for a lighter tone, she said, "You should be especially careful about your omens, Captain. Doughty told me how you broke your statue of Saint Nicholas. I am glad mine is made of wood."

"Yours? You pay homage to the patron saint of sailors?"

"Not merely sailors." She told him of the legend of Saint Nicholas and the unmarried ladies.

"The protector of both maidens and sailors?" Trent said with a lift of his brow. "It would seem old Saint Nick spreads himself a little thin."

"Saints often must do double duty. There are not so many of them." Chloe scarce knew what nonsense she was talking. She was only aware of Trent standing far too near her in the semidarkness. Her heart beat with desires wild and strange, and she felt overwhelmed with guilt, conscious as she was of Emma slumbering behind her, so innocent and trusting. How wicked I am, Chloe thought with despair. If she were to be boiled alive in one of Emma's puddings, it would be no more than she deserved.

Nervously, she snatched up another transparency. "Here's one we haven't seen yet. 'Tis one of my favorites, the wizard in his lair."

But Trent stepped in front of the lantern, the colored light spilling over the crisp white of his cravat and the lean contours of his face, bathing him in a rainbow array at odds with the sorrow in his eyes.

"Something is making you most unhappy," he said. "I almost thought I saw tears swimming in your eyes." He reached out to cup her chin, his fingers firm and warm against her skin. "Can you not tell me what troubles you? I thought we had become friends."

The tenderness in his voice almost proved her undoing. She longed to catch his hand, pillow her cheek against its masculine strength. She shied away, essaying an awkward laugh. "I am merely being foolish. 'Tis only because it is New Year's Eve. It always makes me a little melancholy. 'Tis rather a strange night, you must admit. One tick of the clock and another year slips silently away."

"I understand," he said. "I often feel that way myself. The old year passing, and who knows what disasters the next might bring?"

"It could prove a better year than the one before."

"Or it could be worse."

"But it might be better," she insisted, finding a need to believe that more than ever before. Her voice nearly broke, and she was horrified to feel her eyes stinging. Much to her relief, Lucy and Lathrop returned to the parlor.

"Enough of that dratted lantern and this gloomy darkness," Lucy called out.

"Nay," Lathrop murmured suggestively, "I am rather fond of darkness myself."

Lucy giggled, and Chloe Anne heard her administering a playful rap. Whatever Lathrop had been whispering to her, Lucy's face glowed more brightly than the candles she was lighting.

As the room slowly filled with light, Chloe saw that Trent had already moved away from her side. Like her, he looked ill-disposed for any merriment. But neither her silence nor Will's made any impression upon Lucy.

"Do pack all those things away, Chloe Anne," Lucy said gaily. " 'Tis almost time to see in the new year. Someone must wake poor Emmy, and shall we chase Charles outside to be the first footer?"

Never had Chloe been less inclined to take delight in any of the old legends, but both Trent and Lathrop looked so puzzled, she felt compelled to explain. "What Lucy means is that great care must be taken after midnight that the first person to enter the house in the new year should be fair rather than dark, or else—"

"I know," Trent interrupted with a grimace. "Or else, more bad luck."

"I think we should send Lucy out to be the first footer," Lathrop said. "She is obviously the fairest of us all."

"It cannot be a woman, you fool," Lucy retorted, somehow making even that epithet sound as tender as if she had called him her darling. Lathrop regarded her adoringly.

Their happiness was so obvious, a happiness Chloe realized she would never know. She felt obliged to look away. She had never been inclined to envy her beautiful older sister, at least not until now.

Chloe was on the verge of excusing herself when the clock chimed out the hour of midnight. Emma started, awake, then blushed, apologizing for having dozed off. Lathrop poured out glasses of sherry and passed them round to drink a toast to the new year. Chloe barely tasted hers, and she could not help noting that Will hardly drank his.

She had no sooner settled her glass upon the tray when the parlor door burst open. Polly rushed into the room. The little maid appeared flushed, and she bobbed a hasty curtsy to Will. "Captain Trent. Begging your pardon, sir. But there's a dark-haired stranger come banging at the door, asking for you."

"Dark hair? Oh, no!" Lucy cried with comical dismay.

"We are doomed." Lathrop tossed down the rest of his drink. "Come kiss me, ladies, one last time, before we all perish."

"Charles! Decidedly you have had too much wine," Trent said, then turned back to Polly. "Who the deuce would be calling upon us at this hour of night? Did you not think to ask his name, girl?"

"N-nay, I was that flustered, sir. But the gentleman is wearing a naval uniform."

Trent started a little at that, then excused himself. He moved unhurriedly from the parlor, no apparent urgency in his step. Yet he left an aura of tension in his wake. Even Lathrop and Lucy's merriment faded.

"Oh, dear," Emma said. "Who do you suppose it could be?"

No one even hazarded a guess. Chloe was gripped by a feeling of dread she could not explain. Gathering up her skirts, she rushed out of the parlor. She reached the hall in time to see Trent flinging the door open wider to admit the stranger.

"No, don't," she almost cried out, but she knew Will would feel she was being foolish beyond permission. Perhaps she was, but she found herself shivering as she watched the tall, dark sailor step across the threshold and salute Trent.

"Sorry to arrive so late, sir," the man was saying. "But I have been riding like the devil to bring you these orders from the Admiralty."

He handed over a folded document, affixed with a very official-looking seal.

Chloe held her breath as Trent broke the seal. He stepped to one side, perusing the notice. Whatever the contents, Trent's only reaction was a slight tightening of his mouth.

"What is it, Trent?" Lathrop called out.

Chloe became aware that the others had also filed out from the parlor, but she could not tear her eyes from Will's rigid features.

"Ill tidings, I am afraid," he said. "The rest of my leave has been canceled. I am to report back to Portsmouth as soon as possible. It would seem the *Gloriana*'s refitting has gone much quicker than expected, and her services are needed."

"B-but why? Where will they s-send you?" Chloe stammered.

"I rarely ever know that until I have actually put to sea. I will receive further orders then."

"Do you think there will be another Trafalgar?"

Trent hastened to reassure her. "I doubt my ship will be facing anything so grim as that. Napoleon will never manage to land his army in England, that I promise you. You and your sisters will be quite safe."

Chloe pressed her hand to her lips. It was not *her* safety that she was worried about. It was borne in upon her as never before the dangers Will might face when he left Windhaven. She felt as though a great weight were pressing upon her heart, but she managed a quavery smile. "I . . . I did warn you it was bad luck to let a dark-haired stranger in first."

His answering smile was rather sad.

Lucy, as usual, was concerned with more immediate matters. She frowned. "Does this mean Emma's wedding will have to be postponed?"

Chloe was ashamed to feel a stirring of hope, a hope that swiftly died when Will said, "No, that will not be necessary. We will simply move the ceremony forward to tomorrow, if that is all right with you, madam?" He deferred to Emma, who nodded.

"I shall be ready," she said. Then she moved to make the tired young sailor welcome, inviting him to come down to the kitchens for something to eat.

Chloe could only stare at her sister, marveling at her composure.

"I'd best start making preparations for my journey at once," Will said. He straightened his shoulders, looking like a man preparing for action. "Mr. Doughty must be informed. Polly, be a good lass and go up and bang on his door."

Instead of hastening to obey, Polly stood nervously twisting her apron.

"Polly, did you not hear me?" Trent said more sharply.

"I fear it would do no good, sir." Polly's face puckered. To everyone's astonishment, she burst into tears.

"I can't fetch Mr. Doughty," she blurted out. "He-he's gone."

Chapter 8

It was a foul beginning to the new year, Trent thought. His eyes raw from lack of sleep, he strode along the main lane leading into Littledon, the cobblestoned street of the tiny fishing village glistening wet with melting snow. The scattering of cottages and handful of shops appeared to be slumbering in the chill morning light, even St. Andrew's Church still and silent.

But only moments before, the street had rung with the clatter of horses' hooves, the tromp of booted feet, and the enthusiastic voices of the men who had assembled to begin the search for Mr. Samuel Doughty. Most of these volunteers had come from the farms of the local squire, who was also the district's magistrate. Squire Daniels himself had ridden with them as eagerly as though it were all but sport, more entertaining than any fox hunt.

The boisterous man had even winked at Trent and suggested a reward be posted. "The lads would search a deal harder at the prospect of earning a few bobs."

"The fact that they are serving His Majesty's Royal Navy should be reward enough," had been Trent's frigid reply. It might be his responsibility to attempt the recapture of Doughty, but he was damned if he was going to put a price on the man's head.

His spirits not in the least dampened by Trent's rebuke, the squire led out his men with a loud "halloa," a call that was answered with a chorus of lusty cheers. Only Trent had stood by, grimly silent, as he faced the most onerous duty of any captain, steeling himself to enforce the rigid laws, which demanded severe punishment for any deserter.

When the last of the squire's riders had vanished down the turning of the lane, Trent lingered in the quiet street and cursed Doughty's folly. Even more, he cursed himself for not keeping careful watch over one he had known to be an incorrigible rogue. Why had he ever been so stupid as to bring Doughty away from the ship in the first place? Anger surged through Trent anew. If the rascal was overtaken, Trent was prepared to put his hands about the man's throat and cheerfully throttle him.

Except that he would not have to. The navy would take care of that for him. A sick feeling crawled into the pit of Trent's stomach. He'd seen men hang before, kicking, struggling, turning black in the face unless they were fortunate enough to snap their necks at once.

As William Trent, captain of His Majesty's Royal Navy, it was his duty to press for just such an end to Doughty's crime. But the image kept rising into his mind of Doughty's insouciant grin, and he felt iced through to the marrow of his bones. It was a weakness in him, he knew, but plain Will Trent, the man, kept hoping that somehow the jovial seaman might manage to escape.

As near as Trent had been able to tell from the hysterical Polly, Doughty had slipped away sometime during the supper hour last evening. The silly wench had helped him pack, sneaking him extra rations from the kitchen. Between her hiccuping sobs, Trent gathered that the rascal had promised to return someday and marry Polly. Her and half a dozen other foolish maids wherever Doughty chanced to make port, Trent thought wryly. But the girl had been wailing loudly enough, so Trent had refrained from telling her that.

Doughty had an early-enough start; there was a chance that he could put a goodly distance between himself and Littledon. But Trent couldn't help reflecting that the steward would have been doing most of his traveling in the bitter cold of night most likely on foot. No horses had been taken from Windhaven, and as near as could be determined, none had vanished from any of the outlying farms either. Doughty was a resourceful rogue, but there was a chance he had already met with misfortune in the dark and was lying in a ditch somewhere halffrozen, easy prey.

It was the most damnable dilemma. Trent could not wish Doughty "Godspeed," nor could he hope for his capture either. Never had he been so torn between his duty and his natural inclinations.

Yet it availed him nothing, kicking his heels about the streets, debating the matter. Other things—his imminent departure and arranging the wedding for that afternoon—also required his attention.

His mood as black as the long cape flashing about his ankles, Trent set off for the church. He felt grateful for the silence of the street, in no humor for any company. It was a gratitude he did not experience for long.

At the turning of the lane, the figure of a man in a high-crowned hat came into view. Close at his side was a young woman bundled in a green coat, the ends of her flowing brown hair blowing loose from her bonnet.

Lathrop and Chloe Anne. Trent gritted his teeth and swore. The last thing he needed right now was to gaze into Chloe's beseeching eyes.

Trent gave them no opportunity to approach. Picking up his pace, he headed them off at the top of the lane.

"What the blazes are you doing here, Charles?" he snapped. "I told all of you that it was best to remain at the house. There is nothing any of you can do in this wretched business about Mr. Doughty."

"I haven't come about Doughty," Lathrop said. "I tried to tell you earlier, Trent. I need to consult you on a personal matter."

"Did that make it necessary to drag Chloe Anne out on a morning like this? She already looks frozen through."

Although Chloe was shivering, she made haste to disclaim. "I-I am not in the least cold, and Ch-Charles didn't drag me. I came on my own, to bring some jellies to Peggety and Mrs. Green." As if to make this thin tale more convincing, she displayed the covered basket she balanced on one arm.

Trent glared. "I doubt Mrs. Green has a pressing need for jam at this early hour, and, Charles, at the moment I have no time to attend to any 'personal matters.' The pair of you can just turn around and march straight back to Windhaven."

Intending to give them no chance to argue, Trent started to stride away, but Lathrop caught his arm in a tight grip.

"Dash it, Trent. I know you are preoccupied with Doughty's desertion, but I have to talk to you.

There may not be another chance, and it's extremely important."

Checked by his friend's earnest tone, Trent paused. Although he shook free of Lathrop's grasp, he demanded, "Well, what is it?"

To his astonishment Lathrop blushed like a maid. Summoning a lopsided smile, he said, "You are not the only one who wants to get married.'

Trent arched one brow. Just what the devil was that supposed to mean? Chloe began to murmur some excuse and sidle away, but Lathrop stopped her, drawing her back to his side. "No, Chloe, stay. There is no reason you should not hear this as well."

Taking a deep breath, Lathrop looked Trent straight in the eye. "I want your permission to pay my addresses to your ward."

Trent stared at Lathrop and Chloe, both of them eyeing him so expectantly.

"You mean to Chloe?" he asked, feeling as if he had just taken a kick to the gut.

"Of course not," Chloe Anne said. "He means Lucy. He wants your permission to marry Lucy."

"Yes! Yes, that's it exactly." Lathrop beamed, looking exceedingly grateful for Chloe Anne's help.

Although an odd sensation of relief coursed through Trent, it did nothing to improve his temper. He said sharply, "What utter nonsense, Lathrop. You and Lucy barely know each other."

"We are as well acquainted as you and Emma. At least our courtship was not conducted through correspondence."

"But my engagement is founded upon common sense," Trent said. "Not some holiday flirtation."

Lathrop's eyes flashed. "It isn't like that at all,

Trent. I am in love with Lucy. I will be to the end of my days."

"And Lucy has also formed a lasting attachment to Charles," Chloe put in. "I can assure you of that, Captain."

Trent raked them both with an impatient glare. "No one falls in love in only one week."

He was surprised to see that his remark had caused Chloe Anne to flinch. Lathrop drew himself up into a posture of wounded dignity.

"Do I understand you, then, to be refusing your permission, sir?"

"Don't be an ass, Charles. Of course I am not. I am only asking you and Lucy to show some good sense and take more time before rushing into anything."

"There is no more time," Lathrop said desperately. "You are leaving today. How am I to seek your permission when you are gone to sea? It could be months, years before you return, if ever."

"Then if I don't return, there will be nothing to stand in the way of your happiness, Charles."

"Blast it all, Trent! You know I didn't mean . . . No one would be more grieved than I if anything were to . . ." Lathrop removed his hat, dragging his fingers through his wavy hair in sheer frustration. "I know you have never been in love, Trent, but can you not just try to comprehend?"

"No!" Trent did not know why Lathrop's words should sting him so, but they did. Damn it all to hell. It was Charles who understood nothing. Trent had spent half the night and all of the morning weighing a man's life in the balance. All talk of weddings, including his own, seemed trivial by comparison.

He snarled. "I have enough other difficulties to

177

deal with. I have no patience at the moment for permitting a pair of infatuated fools to take some disastrous step."

Lathrop pressed his lips into a taut white line. His eyes roiled with hurt and anger. But he said quietly, "If that is your final word then, sir, I shall opportune you no further."

Turning stiffly, he offered his arm to Chloe Anne, who had been biting her lips during this entire exchange, her face a picture of silent misery.

"Come, Chloe Anne," Lathrop said. "I will escort you to Mrs. Green's cottage."

"Thank you, but you go on ahead, Charles. I will catch up with you. I need a moment to speak to Captain Trent."

"As you wish, my dear." Lathrop bowed and walked away, refusing to even look at Trent.

Trent felt his own anger sharpened by regret and exasperation. He folded his arms across his chest, knowing he was about to face a far worse barrage on his emotions from Chloe Anne. As soon as Lathrop was out of earshot, Trent attempted to cut her off, saying in harsh accents, "Chloe Anne, if you mean to plead for Charles's suit, you are wasting—"

"Oh, no," she hastened to disclaim. "This isn't about Charles and Lucy, although I do think . . . But never mind that for now. I wanted to speak to you about Polly."

"Polly?" Trent was astonished into relaxing his guard a little.

"Yes, the poor girl is terrified out of her wits. She thinks you will turn her off without a character for helping Mr. Doughty escape."

"Is that all that's troubling you? Tell the silly

chit to stop fretting. She is in no danger of losing her post."

"Thank you. She will be so glad to hear that." Chloe gave him a grateful look, but her bright smile quickly wavered. "Um . . . there is one other thing."

"Don't, Chloe Anne," Trent said. But she was already fixing him with those wide, pleading blue eyes.

"Can you not just call off the search and let Mr. Doughty go?" she whispered.

"You know I cannot."

"But you are his captain."

"Which means that I am more bound by the law than any other man. Do you think I want to see Doughty hang? He is the best steward I have ever had."

"And your friend!" Chloe cried.

"A captain cannot have friends," Trent said bitterly. "And even if he were my best friend in all the world, I still could not countenance his desertion. If it became known that I just looked the other way, I would lose the respect of my entire crew. More than one man's life depends upon the discipline I can maintain aboard my ship. It is important that . . ." His words trailed away as he despaired of ever finding a way to make her understand. He concluded wearily, "Please, Chloe Anne. Don't make this any more difficult for me than it already is."

She said nothing, her eyes dark and troubled. Trent feared that at any moment, she would reproach him bitterly or simply turn her back upon him and walk away. But although she looked far from comprehending, she did neither.

She reached up and touched his cheek. "Go home

and rest as soon as you can, Will," she said gently. "You look very tired."

Astonished but grateful, Trent caught her hand. Turning it over, he found the area of her wrist left exposed by her glove and pressed a brusque kiss there. Finding himself unable to say another word, he stalked away, heading for the churchyard gate.

He had no way of knowing that Chloe Anne's heart went with him. She watched his rapid retreat through a mist of tears. Perhaps she did not fully comprehend the duties of a naval captain, but the anguish in Will's face had been all too clear. She wanted so badly to rush after him.

She always longed to soothe away the woes of those she loved, to make everything all better. The realization that she could not always do so had been one of the most bitter lessons of her life.

Dashing the salt drops from her eyes, she watched until Will disappeared around the side of the church. Then she hurried to catch up with Charles. He was lingering disconsolately in front of the linen draper's shop. The window was still decorated with its sprays of holly. The festive greenery seemed somehow a hollow mockery, a reminder of a day when they had all felt so much happier than now.

Charles said not a word as she approached, merely offered her his arm. In a most despondent silence, they set off together to seek out Mrs. Green's cottage.

It was nearly half an hour later when Trent emerged from the rectory, his business concluded. Mr. Henry had paled a little at Trent's request, but he had made no difficulty whatsoever about moving the wedding forward to that afternoon.

Trent almost wished that the vicar had complained. Doughty's defection had left Trent so shaken, he no longer felt sure of anything. His marriage to Emma had seemed such a sensible course, but now he didn't know.

As he made his way past the churchyard gate, he brought himself up short with a brisk shake. It was far too late to be harboring any such qualms. The best he could do was to hasten back to Windhaven and tell Emma that she needed to be ready for the ceremony by a quarter to five.

Yet he could not seem to urge his feet into movement. He felt loath to return to Windhaven, dreading the prospect that the squire might already be there, gleefully dragging Doughty along like a hunter's trophy, trussed and bound.

As unlikely as that was to happen so soon, Trent was equally reluctant to face a household of chattering women. In his present humor, there was only one lady whose company he desired.

Rather wistfully, he gazed up the street where he had seen Chloe last, although he realized she would have been long gone. He was correct. There was no sign of her. But Lathrop was in full view, nearly knocking down some shopkeeper who was unlocking his front door. Hatless, Lathrop rushed on, not even pausing to apologize. He came tearing down the street like a madman.

By the time he reached Trent, he was white-faced, breathless. Gripping the front of Trent's coat, Lathrop stared at him with wild eyes.

"Charles! What the devil's amiss?" Trent felt a shaft of dread pierced him. "Chloe Anne! Has something happened to her?"

Lathrop managed to shake his head. "B-baby," he gasped.

"What?" Trent said, feeling he could not have heard correctly.

"Baby!" Lathrop fairly roared. "That . . . that infernal Green woman is having her baby."

Relief flooded through Trent. For the first time that morning, he felt an urge to smile. "Calm yourself, Charles," he said, prying his friend's clutching hands from his cloak. "It is a natural consequence when a woman becomes that . . . er . . . interesting."

"But the baby! It's coming all by itself."

"It is my understanding that they usually do, Charles."

Lathrop eyed him reproachfully. "This is no time for jesting, Trent. Chloe Anne is back there at that cottage with a woman who is going to give birth at any moment, and there is only a three-year-old to help."

"What!" Trent scowled. "You left Chloe alone with a woman in labor?"

"What was I supposed to do? Chloe told me to go fetch the midwife. Where the deuce does one go to get a midwife?" Lathrop cried, looking distractedly about him as though at any moment he might start turning over the rocks themselves in his search.

Trent thought rapidly. "Go to the rectory and ask for Mr. Henry. If anyone would know where the midwife is to be found, it would be him. And do strive for a little more coherency, Charles."

"And just what the blazes are you going to do?" Lathrop demanded indignantly.

"I am going down to the cottage to help Chloe Anne."

Lathrop gaped at him. "You are going to try to deliver a baby?"

"I don't know what the devil I am going to do.

But the next time I am ever tempted to take leave from the sanity of my ship, shoot me!"

After this savage request, Trent rushed off down the street himself. He had been to the Greens' cottage only once before. But in a village the size of Littledon, there was no difficulty about finding the place again.

The cottage did not rest in the village proper but nestled on the outskirts, farther down the beach. As his boots crunched over the pebbled surface, Trent glimpsed the outline of a cold gray sea lapping the shore.

Yet despite its bleak setting, the small stone dwelling presented a cozy appearance, wisps of smoke swirling up from its chimney. An aura of serenity enveloped the cottage, heedless of the sea winds buffeting the whitewashed walls and rattling the shutters.

Yet when Trent raised his fist to hammer upon the wooden door, he detected the sound of a high-pitched wailing from within. Growing more anxious, he barely waited for a response before knocking again.

The door was flung open, and a distraught-looking Chloe appeared on the threshold, balancing Peggety on her hip. The child had obviously been crying, but she subsided, pillowing her tear-stained face against Chloe's shoulder and earnestly sucking on two fingers.

Chloe looked on the verge of tears herself. "Oh, Will!" she choked. "I am so very glad you have come. Did you bring the midwife with you?"

"No, I am afraid not," Trent said, easing Chloe and the child back out of the doorway, then shutting out the fierce wind. He blinked to adjust his eyes to the darkened interior, the cottage's tiny windows affording little light. Only the fire crackling upon the hearth served to illuminate the room's meager furnishings: a table and two chairs, a wooden stool, a small cot, and a curtained doorway leading into another room.

As Trent focused upon Chloe Anne's delicate features, he saw her eyes brimming with despair. He made haste to reassure her. "Everything will be all right. I sent Charles to see Mr. Henry. I am sure the two of them will locate the midwife and be here in a trice."

Chloe shook her head. "They will be too late."

"Nonsense," Trent said. His reassurance was already belied by a frantic cry coming from the next room.

For a moment, Chloe's shoulders slumped. Then she straightened, shifting Peggety slightly in her arms. Chloe raised her head, tilting up her stubborn chin.

"I shall just have to help Mrs. Green myself," she announced.

"What! But, Chloe Anne, how would you know—" Trent started to protest, but she interrupted, saying, "Here! You must look after Peggety."

To his horror, Chloe thrust the child into his arms. Trent balanced her as stiffly as though he held a block of wood. Peggety removed her fingers from her mouth and began to howl.

"What the deuce am I to do with her?" Trent asked, but Chloe Anne had already vanished behind the curtain into the next room.

"Chloe Anne!" He started to follow but drew up short. Somehow that thin curtain, veiling as it did such solemn female mysteries, was a far more daunting prospect than any enemy vessel he had ever attempted to board. Damning himself for a coward, he could not bring himself to go barging in there. Never in his life had he felt so blasted helpless.

But another earsplitting wail from Peggety forced him to focus on his most immediate problem.

"Hush, hush," he said, sinking down onto the stool, jiggling the child ineffectually on his knee.

Peggety regarded him reproachfully through the tumble of her curls, her plump lower lip atremble. "Warnt Marmar. Warnt Marmar."

"You shall have your mama presently," Will said, pausing his vigorous bouncing in some astonishment. By God, he had actually managed to understand something the child said. Feeling considerably heartened, he resumed the bouncing, but Peggety apparently failed to understand that some sort of diplomatic breakthrough had been reached. She continued to cry.

Trent racked his memory for anything he had ever heard about children. What did one do with a crying babe? Rock her? Tell her stories? That sounded vaguely as though it might have some merit. Though he scarce knew what he was going to tell the weeping child, Trent drew in a deep breath and plunged in.

"Once upon a time . . ." he began desperately, praying that Charles would arrive with that midwife very soon.

It could not have been more than an hour later, but Chloe felt as if she had spent all day closeted with Sukey Green in the cramped, gloomy quarters of the bedchamber. Her head tossing against the pillow, her damp curls so like Peggety's, Sukey looked achingly young herself. She gripped Chloe's hand hard, pressing her lips together in a valiant effort to stifle her cries while her babe struggled to be born.

But by the time the midwife finally arrived, another cry was heard, softer, like the mew of a kitten. The old woman bustled in, elbowing Chloe aside. The midwife had a crooked nose and breath reeking of garlic, but she set to work with practiced hands. After such an unendurable vigil, it seemed that in no time at all, Sukey rested with a small bundle tucked into her arms, the face of her infant son peeking from the folds of the blanket. Chloe, her limbs shaking with relief, sagged down on the end of the bed.

"Bless me." The old woman cackled. "What a new year this has turned out to be. Wasn't I just finishing with the birthing of Mrs. Catesby's wee girl when round comes the vicar to fetch me. But you lasses appear to have been managing quite nicely. Quite nicely, indeed." She bestowed a toothy grin on Chloe. " 'Tis all over and done, miss. So don't you go aswooning on me now."

"I wasn't about to," Chloe said indignantly, forcing herself to her feet, although she did feel a little wobbly. "I *have* helped at a confinement before, when our old dog whelped her puppies."

The old woman slapped her knee and roared with laughter, but Sukey gave Chloe a wan, grateful smile.

"Thank you so much, Miss Chloe. I don't know what I would have done if you hadn't come round. There is only one more thing. My Tom. I must get a letter to him, tell him about the boy."

"I am sure Captain Trent will know how to get a dispatch to your husband as soon as possible," Chloe Anne said soothingly.

But even as she gave this assurance, Chloe recollected guiltily in what case she had left Will. With a sobbing three-year-old in his arms, the captain might not be feeling particularly obliging.

"Don't be fretting about letters 'n' such just now, dearie," the midwife scolded Sukey. "You are exhausted. Miss Chloe, would you mind tending to the babe while I get Mrs. Green settled more comfortable-like?"

Chloe was only too happy to comply with this request. With a tired sigh, Sukey kissed her son's cheek before Chloe scooped the warm bundle into her arms. His small face had that newborn scrubbed-red look, but Chloe thought him quite the most handsome creature she had ever seen.

He already showed signs of being a most saintly child, for the moment content to doze as though he, too, had found the ordeal of being born quite exhausting. Cooing softly to the babe, Chloe prepared with some trepidation to step into the next room and see how Will was faring.

As she nudged the curtain aside, Chloe heard the low drone of his voice. Will was talking to someone, perhaps the vicar, or maybe even Charles had come.

But when she slipped across the threshold, Chloe was puzzled to see no one else present but Peggety. Will had to be addressing the child. Staring into the fire, he did not seem to realize that Peggety had fallen asleep in his arms. Snuggling the babe securely against her, Chloe inched forward, trying to make sense of what Will was saying.

"And the captain knew the folly of pursuing such a course in a squall, but he was a most stubborn man. When the storm reached the pitch of its fury, he called to his first mate, 'Prepare to abandon ship.' 'Aye, aye, sir,' the mate replied, roaring out to the crew above the wail of the storm, 'Say your prayers, ye lubbers, for I fear we are all about to meet our Maker.' "

Chloe listened in astonishment, her lips curved into a smile. A story. He was telling Peggety some kind of story.

"The waves washed over the deck, and the masthead came crashing down. All seemed lost, but at that moment a miracle occurred. As though she had heard the captain's cry, the beautiful lady of the sea came rising up from the ocean's floor. With gentle hands, she quieted the waves, and—"

Regrettably at that moment a floorboard creaked, betraying Chloe's presence. Will glanced around, and his face flushed a dull red.

"Oh, don't stop now," Chloe said. "You must tell me what happened. Did the lady save the stubborn captain?"

"Likely so," Trent said gruffly. "The fellow was far too obstinate to drown." He shifted carefully, peering down at the sleeping Peggety, her breath coming in soft, contented sighs. The trusting way the child nestled against Trent's broad chest brought a curious lump to Chloe Anne's throat.

" 'Twas all but a pack of nonsense," he said. "But at least I seem to have bored our young friend here to sleep."

"To dream of three-masted ships and jolly Jack-Tars, no doubt."

"She *is* a sailor's daughter," Will said. "What else should she dream about?" He struggled to his feet, taking great care lest he disturb Peggety. He settled the child upon the cot in the corner of the room. She curled up at once, somehow guiding her two fingers to her mouth even in the depths of slumber. Will tucked the blanket around her and after a brief hesitation patted the little girl's curls, the gesture both awkward and tender.

He straightened, keeping his voice low as he asked, "Is Mrs. Green all right? I mean, did all go well in there?"

"See for yourself. Peggety has a new brother."

Trent started, becoming aware that the bundle clutched so protectively in Chloe's arms was a baby. As she drew closer, Trent took a polite but cautious peek in much the same manner he might have viewed some curious variety of sea life.

"Here, you hold him," Chloe said with her customary impulsiveness.

Trent retreated a hasty step. "Oh, no. I only recently mastered the art of keeping a grip on a squirming three-year-old. I would prefer to work my way down in rank more gradually."

But there was no gainsaying Chloe Anne. She shoved the babe into his arms with a silvery laugh. "Don't look so terrified. He won't break."

"Won't he, indeed?" Trent muttered. After he had held Peggety's sturdy little frame, the babe felt as fragile and weightless as a china teacup. Trent risked one awestruck glance beneath the blanket. He had never known human beings could come in such tiny form. A golden dusting of hair crowned the little one's head, almost invisible lashes resting against soft cheeks. One diminutive hand stirred against the blanket folds. It was almost enough to make a man believe in such things as fairies.

When his wondering gaze at last drifted up to meet Chloe's, he saw that her eyes were aglow with such pride and tenderness, it could have been her own babe she presented. He imagined she would look just so someday when she offered up her first-born son to her husband.

A bittersweet longing shot through him as he held the babe, bathed in the glow of Chloe's gentle smile. From some great distance, he could hear the wind beating against the cottage. But for one moment he felt strangely bound to Chloe in some safe harbor, far removed from the elements, removed from time itself as he stood there imagining that not only might this be her babe, but his. Except—

Except that if he ever had a son, he would likely be far away at sea, just like Tom Green was when the little lad was born. And Chloe Anne would not be the mother of his child.

He handed the babe back to her, filled with a regret as keen as it was unexplainable. "We had best be going," he said. "The vicar stopped by here for a few minutes to tell me that Charles went back to Windhaven to fetch the carriage for us. It looks like there is going to be a storm."

Chloe nodded with a tiny sigh. Slipping into the other room, Trent could hear her handing the infant over to the midwife. Trent helped Chloe into her coat, then held the door for her.

Any words they might have spoken would have been snatched away by the brisk wind, but neither of them seemed to have anything to say. Lost in silence, they trudged back along the shingled beach.

Chloe Anne's bonnet blew back, hanging by its strings, her hair becoming a wild tangle. Shielding her eyes, she stared out to sea. When she spoke, Trent had to lean closer to catch her words.

"I like the look of a beach in the morning. Everything is washed clean and new as though it were a chance to begin again. The birth of a baby is something like that, too, isn't it?" She paused to glance up at him. "I mean, no matter how terrible things might seem, it is still the beginning of a new life, new hopes."

"I suppose so," Trent agreed, though he scarce knew what he was saying. It suddenly occurred to him that long after he returned to his ship, in the lonely hours standing watch on deck, he would be seeing her this way, her honey brown hair blowing in the wind, her lips softly smiling, her light blue eyes always so wistful with dreaming.

He would see her everywhere, in the foaming waves, in the night sky, in the crisp billow of the sail as it sang in the wind. Somehow she was in his heart now as much as the sea itself.

His hands came up to grip her shoulders, and he began drawing her forward. He wanted nothing so much as to clasp her in his arms, to hold her fast forever. The desire came upon him as strong and fierce as the gathering storm.

He heard Chloe give a soft gasp, but she didn't resist. What he saw reflected in the depths of her eyes fairly took his breath away. He would have kissed her then, but she ducked her head, and his lips merely grazed her forehead.

Somehow he retained enough sanity to release her. Reaching up, he drew her bonnet back over her head. As he secured the ribbons at her chin, tying them in a bow that was most militarily precise, he noted how badly his fingers were trembling.

Chloe caught his hand between her own. "Will, I-I ..." she began, then stopped, her face full of despair. "I suppose we had best hurry. Emma will be worried about us."

"Yes," he said hoarsely. She released his hand and turned, fairly running up the beach. Trent watched her for a moment, stifling a soft curse.

It was a poor time to be realizing such a thing only hours away from his own wedding. But he was about to marry the wrong sister.

Chapter 9

As afternoon shadows lengthened, the entire Windhaven household gathered in little St. Andrew's Church for Miss Emma's wedding. Even though the ceremony had yet to begin, Old Meg was already reaching sentimentally for her handkerchief. Polly sniffed gustily, though no one was sure whether it was over the present occasion or the absence of Mr. Doughty.

The steward had thus far eluded capture, much to Chloe Anne's relief. At least his arrest would not cast any further pall over a wedding day that already seemed lost in gloom. The gray clouds without had brought on an early darkness, causing the sexton to scurry about, lighting more candles.

The storm that had threatened all afternoon had yet to break, but the wind could still be heard setting up a mournful wail. Sitting in the front pew, Chloe Anne shivered a little, her heart feeling as heavy as the overburdened skies.

The rest of her family appeared no more cheerful than she. They might well have been attending a funeral service instead of a marriage. Attired in her best bonnet and gown, a pale Emma stood before the altar, her nervousness betrayed by the fluttering of her hands. Lucy and Lathrop were the picture of misery. Situated across the aisle from each other, they exchanged longing glances.

The only one at all composed was Agnes, staring vacantly up at a stained-glass window. But then her mind was likely far away, daydreaming about some musty old Romans.

Lucy fidgeted on the seat beside Chloe and whispered in peevish accents, "What is taking the captain and Mr. Henry so long? What else could Trent possibly have to say to him?"

"Perhaps there is some last-minute detail that has been overlooked," Chloe said. She had no more notion what might be causing the delay than Lucy did, but she stood fiercely ready to defend any of Will's actions.

Lucy scowled. "Doesn't the captain think Mr. Henry knows his own business? You were right about Trent all along, Chloe Anne. He is a high-handed, interfering tyrant."

"He is nothing of the kind!"

"Oh yes, he is! He cannot give one good reason, yet he is forbidding Charles and me to become engaged."

"As your guardian, Will is obliged to keep you from making a mistake, and—" Chloe ducked her head, adding quietly, "And he does not believe anyone can fall in love that fast."

But there had been one moment back there on the beach when Chloe had questioned the captain's lack of faith. For one moment, when he had drawn her closer, the look in his eyes had spoken not of skepticism, but of a passion as strong and deep as the sea itself. But either Will's common sense had reasserted itself, or it had all been the product of her own wild and wicked imagination. Most likely the latter, Chloe Anne thought.

Lucy stole another wistful look at Charles, then grumbled, "Well, I think Will Trent is a great fool."

"No, he is simply a man who will always adhere to his own notions of duty and honor," Chloe said with simple pride. And she loved him for it, even though it was those selfsame qualities in Will that were likely to break her heart.

She inched farther away from Lucy, not wanting to hear any more of her criticisms. Chloe knew she would have enough to do simply to put on a brave front, to be able to offer Will and Emma her congratulations. Her only hope was that given time, perhaps the strength of her feelings for Will would fade to become something more sisterly. It was a poor consolation, but all she had. In the meantime, she could only wish that Trent would come with Mr. Henry and make an end of this ordeal.

In the small robing room behind the altar, that was precisely what Trent was trying to do. While Mr. Henry donned his vestments, Trent paced the cramped quarters. Clad in the full regalia of his best uniform, he felt more like he was about to plunge into battle than into wedlock. Which perhaps he was—a battle for the only happiness he might ever know.

Chloe Anne had always been so certain that Emma and Mr. Henry were still in love with each other. Trent had his doubts, but he prayed fervently that Chloe's instincts might prove more accurate than his own. If she were wrong . . .

No, he could not consider that prospect. It was far too bleak.

Clearing his throat, Trent launched his first tentative barrage, heaping praises upon Mr. Henry until the poor young vicar turned quite pink.

"And never have I been so moved as by your sermons. Such clarity of thought, such force of expression."

Mr. Henry looked as though he thought Trent quite mad, but he said politely, "Indeed? It is heartening to know someone stayed awake long enough to listen."

"You are a man of great talents, quite wasted upon this tiny parish. You should be in possession of a much better living, and I intend to see to that."

"You . . . you overwhelm me, sir. I scarce know what to say."

"Say nothing but that you will accept my friendship and allow me to exert my influence on your behalf."

"That is most kind of you, but I assure you I am quite undeserving."

"This is no time to be modest," Trent growled. When Mr. Henry shrank back apace, Trent reminded himself that he wasn't browbeating one of his midshipmen. Modifying his tone, he said, "Forgive my impertinence, but I understand that you are charged with the support of your mother and several younger siblings. Think what an improvement in your position could mean to them."

"Well, one does not like to be thought mercenary," Mr. Henry said wistfully. "But a slight raise in income would be most welcome."

"And then you could afford to take a wife." Trent gave the slender vicar a hearty slap on the back. "As Saint Paul said, better to marry than to burn."

Trent watched Mr. Henry's face anxiously, fearing he might have overdone it a bit. He couldn't imagine the quiet vicar even smoldering. But a flicker of something appeared in Mr. Henry's mild eyes.

"Yes, I could marry then, couldn't I?" he said

eagerly. "I have always thought it good for a clergyman to set an example for his flock by choosing a proper bride."

"And there is no lady more proper than Miss Emma Waverly. She would make an excellent vicar's wife."

"Aye, indeed she would—" Mr. Henry began warmly, then stopped, looking deeply self-conscious. His spark of animation died. "But Miss Waverly is betrothed to you, Captain."

"Ladies have been known to change their minds," Trent hinted with mounting desperation. "Emma is such an attractive creature, I would scarce blame you if you were tempted to steal her away at the altar itself."

Mr. Henry drew himself upright, looking outraged, and Trent silently cursed himself, realizing that his last salvo had been a grave misfire.

"Sir!" Mr. Henry said in offended accents. "That is a most dreadful jest. Eloping with your bride! Do you think a respectable lady like Miss Waverly would countenance such behavior?"

"She might find it rather romantic," Trent suggested weakly.

"She would find it reprehensible and the most baseless ingratitude to one who is proposing to become my benefactor."

Trent nearly groaned aloud. Damn his eyes. Why did the vicar have to be so blasted honorable? Trent already felt as if he were strangling upon enough honor for the both of them.

"It is not as if I would be that heartbroken if something happened to stop the wedding," Trent said, trying to sound as callous as possible. "Emma and I scarce know each other. We are virtual strangers."

"In time you will come to realize what a jewel she is, to love her as much as—" The vicar checked himself. Looking extremely noble, he concluded, "We must no longer keep the bride waiting, sir."

Without giving Trent a chance to say any more, Mr. Henry took to his heels, rushing out of the room with as much haste as though he fled the whisperings of the devil.

"Damn! Damn! Damn!" Trent muttered, heedless of the sacred walls surrounding him. He smacked his fist against the wall, wishing it were Mr. Henry's thick head. He would go grab the good vicar by the scruff of his surplice, haul him back here, and . . .

Trent lowered his arm with a weary sigh. No, by God, he'd been a naval captain long enough to know a defeat when he saw it. He had done everything but pick up Emma and thrust her into Mr. Henry's arms, and still, his tactics had utterly failed.

So now what was he going to do? Go out to Emma and say to her, "I am sorry, my dear. I cannot marry you today. I have fallen in love with your sister."

Trent knew how much luck he would have trying to get those words out. Hadn't he already tried to talk to Emma when he had taken Chloe back to Windhaven to prepare for the wedding? How did one say anything so devastating to a woman who was rushing about in an apron tied over her bridal dress, helping to bake the bread for her own wedding supper?

Well, he was about to pay the price for his cowardice in keeping silent. He had failed with Mr. Henry, and there was no approaching Emma now. Trent could hardly jilt her at the altar, humiliate her in front of her family and servants. Even if there was a chance that Chloe Anne would ever return his love, she would never forgive him for hurting her sister. More important, he would never forgive himself.

"Oh, Chloe Anne, Chloe Anne. What a fool I've been," he murmured sadly, knowing that it was the last time he could ever allow himself to pronounce her name with such tenderness.

Well, there was little point in prolonging this agony. Squaring his shoulders, he opened the door and marched out into the nave of the church. Years of rigid close-order drill stood him in good stead, for he looked neither right nor left. Above all else, he feared meeting Chloe Anne's eyes, feared that for once his sense of duty might fail him.

He focused instead upon Emma, who was waiting patiently for him in front of the altar. She was obviously as nervous as any bride might be, but her placid features revealed no great inner distress. Her eyes were quite dry, and she did not even look at Mr. Henry as he opened his prayer book.

Trent moved woodenly to Emma's side, taking her by the hand. She felt quite cold. Or was it his own flesh lacking any warmth?

Dear God, Trent prayed. I've seldom troubled you unless I thought my ship was in danger of sinking. Unless you send a miracle quickly, this time I shall definitely fetch up on the bottom.

The only answer was a silence so vast, Trent could hear the old cook sniffing at the back of the church. Mr. Henry fumbled with the prayer book, and the ceremony began.

As though determined to belie all Trent's praise of him, the young vicar was more than usually awkward, stammering over the words, losing his place in the text.

"If-if anyone knows just cause," he faltered, "why this man and this woman should not—"

Mr. Henry dropped the prayer book. Red-faced, he retrieved it, thumbing through the pages with trembling fingers as he sought to begin again.

"If any man . . . if any man knows . . ." His voice trailed away to nothing. He closed up the book, his eyes meeting Emma's with a look of complete despair. "I am sorry, Emma. I cannot," he whispered. "I simply cannot do this."

All color drained from Emma's face. She struggled for her composure, but for once she seemed unable to keep her heart from surfacing in her eyes. A single tear trickled down her cheek.

Turning to Trent, she hung her head. "I am sorry, too, Captain Trent. I fear I cannot go through with this."

His miracle had come so quietly, Trent was slow to recognize it. When he realized what was happening, his relief was so vast, he was made nigh dizzy by it.

"No need to apologize, my dear," he said, wringing Emma's hand. "No need at all." For the first time in their acquaintance, Trent experienced an urge to grab Emma and plant a hearty kiss on her cheek, and he did so.

A restive murmur ran through the assembled witnesses, and Trent realized Mr. Henry and Emma had spoken so low that very likely no one else understood what was happening.

Turning, he confronted a gathering of astonished faces, but Trent sought out only one. Biting upon her lower lip, Chloe regarded him with anxious eyes.

Stifling an idiotic grin, Trent tried to give his announcement all the gravity the situation demanded. "I am sorry to disappoint you, but—"

It was an announcement he never had the opportunity to finish, for the church door crashed open. At first it seemed as though the heavy portal might have been blown by the wind, but then a burly man rushed in.

Amid astonished cries, Doughty staggered down the aisle, his hair standing up in wild tufts. Breathless with coughing, his face and clothes were streaked with soot.

Any tentative happiness and relief Trent had been feeling were driven from him like the clang of a hammer's blow. Before the steward could manage to choke out a word, Trent charged at him.

"Doughty! You damned villain." Trent seized him by the collar. In a low voice meant for the steward's ears alone, he hissed, "You bloody fool. What the devil possessed you to come back here?"

"H-had to warn you, Cap'n." Doughty wheezed. "F-fire. Me 'n' the groom tried to put it out, but 'tis already out of control."

"Fire! What fire? What the deuce are you talking about? If this is more of your tricks—" Trent said, uneasiness sluicing through him as he noticed that Doughty reeked of smoke.

"No trick, sir. Fire up at the house. Fire at Windhaven."

His rasping words echoed through the church with greater effect than a thunderclap. After a moment of stunned silence, everyone made a mad rush for the door. Trent was the first to cross the threshold, staring off to the west, in the direction of Windhaven Manor.

Even against the gathering darkness, a most unnatural glow lit up the evening sky.

"No. No!" Trent heard a soft cry behind him. It came from Chloe Anne. She plunged wildly past him, darting into the lane as though she would run the mile back to Windhaven on foot if permitted to do so.

Moving swiftly, Trent caught her by the shoulders, gently restraining her. "No," he said. "To the carriage. Quickly."

In her panic, she scarce seemed to comprehend him, but then she nodded. With an efficiency borne of years of command, Trent snapped out orders to Mr. Henry to sound the alarm, telling Lathrop to help bundle the dazed women into the old coach that had been waiting to convey the wedding party back to Windhaven.

As the vehicle lurched through the darkness, Chloe Anne was thrown up against Trent. She clutched at his hand and he sought to offer her some words of assurance, but none came. He had a very bad feeling about this.

His worst fears were realized as the coach turned up the drive. The horses plunged back in such terror that the coachman could no longer drive them on. Flinging open the coach door, Trent dismounted to face the hellish scene taking place before his eyes.

The west wing was already a blazing inferno, the fire leaping toward the sky. And the wind, the merciless wind, only served to fan the flames, driving them toward the main body of the house, as though Windhaven were naught but so much dried tinder.

Momentarily stunned, Trent felt Chloe Anne tugging at his hands.

"Oh, Will, please," she begged, her breath catching in a sob. "Make it stop. Please do something."

Will did not know what was harder to bear, her complete faith in him or his own sense of helplessness. He would have marched into hell itself for her. But he knew nothing he could do this night

was going to save Chloe Anne's beloved Windhaven.

Chloe Anne had always believed that no matter
how great the disaster, things would always look
brighter in the morning. But as she surveyed the
ruin of what had been her home, she wished the
night had never ended, the darkness forever veiling
Windhaven's scarred walls.

The sun would choose today of all days to poke
through the clouds, bringing light but no warmth,
a most merciless light that revealed the west wing
to be nothing but a pile of charred beams. The main
portion of the house remained standing, but the
stonework was scorched black, the stench of smoke
yet strong in the air.

Chloe felt nearly sick from the cloying smell, her
eyes rubbed sore from a night she would never forget yet never clearly remember. The ordeal had already become a blur of images like a bad dream:
the demonic red-gold light of the fire, Windhaven's
timbers crackling and groaning as though the house
itself were crying out in pain. Will's desperate, determined face as he sought to round up all hands
and organize a bucket brigade. But it had all been
hopeless against such raging conflagration, as
hopeless as expecting a single tear to put out the
fires of hell.

Only the storm breaking at last had prevented
Windhaven's burning entirely to the ground. With
a wild crack of thunder, an icy rain had cascaded
down in torrents. But Chloe had been unable to
greet the deluge with a cry of joy. She had stood
numbly, rainwater streaming down her face,
watching the flames expire in an angry hiss, like

some fiery monster in its death throes. But the monster had already done its work.

Chloe vaguely recollected Will's strong hands on her shoulders, forcing her to come away. Everyone had returned to the vicarage to get warm and dry, to await the coming of first light to see how bad the damage had been.

No one had been able to sleep, but Chloe had pretended to do so, not wanting to talk to anyone. She felt as though some bright part of her had been reduced to ashes along with Windhaven, that part of her that had always found reason to hope.

She knew Will's marriage to Emma had been but temporarily disrupted. No doubt the ceremony would be completed in the morning, and then Will would be gone.

When the others had trudged out to view the wreckage, she had joined them out of sheer listlessness, having no real desire to go poking about in the debris, seeing what was to be salvaged of a lifetime of memories.

Her sisters kept stealing wistful glances at her, waiting as though expecting some of her customary good cheer and optimism. Chloe had none left to offer them.

Not that they needed her comfort, in any case. She had already heard them whispering, making plans. The vicarage was far too small. They would have to beg temporary shelter at the squire's manor until arrangements were made to travel to London, to stay with Cousin Harriet. Lathrop had offered to escort them.

That was all well and good for the others. Windhaven had never meant as much to Lucy, Agnes, or even Emma. Chloe's sisters, even Agnes, seemed to understand that, going out of their way to be kind to her.

But Chloe shrank from their sympathy, stealing away at first opportunity to what remained of the blighted garden. Sinking down on the old garden bench, she only wanted to be left alone. Her lips set into a taut line when she saw Agnes approaching.

Her self-assured little sister looked strangely younger this morning. Perhaps owing to the hair tumbled about her pinched face, or because she was wearing a cloak borrowed from Mr. Henry's mama, three sizes too big. With unaccustomed diffidence, she sidled up to Chloe Anne.

"It is not all so bad, really, Chloe," she said in a gruff little voice. "I have been up to our room. The fire went out before it did much damage there, although of course everything reeks of smoke. But look what I fetched down for you."

Extending her hand, she displayed a sooty wooden object. It took Chloe a moment to recognize her small carving of Saint Nicholas. She only stared at it, making no move to take it.

Agnes drew forth a handkerchief and proceeded to ruin the fine linen in an anxious effort to wipe the figure clean. "I knew you would want to take this to London with you."

"Whatever for?" Chloe Anne asked dully.

"Well . . . well, because it's your Saint Nicholas. Your good-luck piece."

"It's only a carved block of old wood," Chloe said.

Hadn't Agnes told Chloe exactly the same thing many times? Then why did the girl look so crestfallen, scrubbing harder than ever at the old figurine?

"There. 'Tis almost as good as new."

When Chloe still did not reach for it, Agnes's

smile faded. She fretted her lip, looking as though she wanted to say something more but didn't know quite what. After an awkward pause, she laid the statue beside Chloe on the bench and walked away with a sad backward glance.

Chloe felt like the greatest wretch imaginable. Agnes must be hurting, too. The library had been gutted, every last one of her precious books gone. Chloe might at least have thanked her little sister, but even that simple gesture seemed to demand too much of her.

Her gaze drifted down to the object on the bench. The statue's wooden eyes, which she had once fancied so wise, stared blankly back at her. An unreasoning surge of anger coursed through her. Chloe snatched up the figure and dashed it to the ground.

Then she buried her face in her hands, wishing more than anything that she could cry. But last night's fire seemed to have consumed every last drop of water, even her own tears.

She did not look up when she heard the crunch of a footfall and sensed a presence looming over her. It had to be Emma hovering again, or perhaps Agnes had come back.

She choked out, "Can not all of you just leave me be?"

"I am afraid I cannot do that, Chloe Anne." Trent's quiet voice penetrated the haze of her misery.

Chloe lowered her hands to peer up at him, his face lined with exhaustion, a strand of dark hair tumbling across his brow. She glimpsed the remains of his once handsome uniform beneath his open cloak, the fabric rumpled, the buttons tarnished, one sleeve slightly scorched. He looked very much like a weary commander returning from battle, one that he had lost.

"I have had no chance to speak with you alone," he said. "And I very much need to do so. May I sit down?"

Chloe merely shrugged. He took this for her consent, lowering himself stiffly to her side.

"I cannot imagine what there is to say," Chloe said bitterly. "Though I suppose I do owe you an apology."

"For what?"

"For burning your house down. You did warn me about the dangers of having those decorations in the parlor."

"The fire had nothing to do with your decorations. It started in the west wing. Your groom thought he heard a prowler. When he went to investigate, he dropped his lantern. But this has not all been a total disaster, Chloe Anne. Luckily, the wind was blowing away from the stables, and the main part of the house—"

"Is a total ruin," Chloe interrupted with a touch of asperity. "There is no need for any of this heartening pretense, Captain. This disaster merely saved you the problem of tearing Windhaven down yourself. I know you never wanted to live here with Emma."

"I admit it freely. I never did. Not with Emma, in any case," he added.

But Chloe rushed on, not heeding him. "Now you can do as you always wanted with a clear conscience, find Emma some smart new house near town."

"Where Emma lives is none of my concern. That is going to be Mr. Henry's problem."

When Chloe stared at him, he said, "Didn't you

understand what took place in church yesterday? My marriage to Emma has been postponed—forever. You were right all along. Mr. Henry and Emma are still in love. The pair of them could have saved us all a deal of trouble by being a little less noble. Emma should have made her feelings known to me at the start."

Astonished and confused, Chloe seemed unable to take in the full import of his words. She focused on his criticism of Emma. "My sister is a perfect lady, Captain Trent. She has always been wonderfully self-contained, never one to make a vulgar parade of her emotions."

"If that is what being a lady means, I wish Mr. Henry joy of her. For my part, I much prefer the girl who wears her heart on her sleeve."

He covered one of Chloe's hands with his own. "My dear, I know this is a poor time to speak of such a thing the day after the dissolution of my engagement to your sister, but . . ." Will paused, swallowing hard. Chloe had never known Trent to be so shy about speaking his mind, but she felt far too drained to offer him any encouragement.

"I wonder," he said, "if you could find it in your heart to consider—just consider, mind you—the prospect of . . . of one day marrying me."

Chloe gasped. Could he possibly have thought of anything more cruel to say to her? She yanked her hand away, crying savagely. "Oh, don't!"

"Then you find the thought that repugnant. I had hoped . . ."

His voice trailed away as Chloe shot to her feet, blazing with hurt and anger. "Go back to your blasted ship, Will. Your duty is finished here. You have seen Emma restored to Mr. Henry, and Lucy is also as good as spoken for. Agnes and I will be taken care of somehow. You need feel under no further obligation to my father's memory."

Flushing, Trent also leapt up. "This has nothing to do with your father. I did not propose to you out of duty. Damn it, Chloe Anne. I . . . I love you."

"No one falls in love in only one week!"

Trent flinched to hear his own heedless words flung back at him. "I was wrong about that, too, and I have already told Charles and Lucy so. They may leave at once for Gretna Green if they've a mind to—with my blessing.

"Perhaps it is asking too much for you to forget what a fool I have been," he said. "I only beg you to believe one thing. I do love you, Chloe Anne."

But as he gazed deep into her lackluster blue eyes, Trent was tormented by the fear that Chloe Anne was never going to believe in anything again. No more fairies, no more ghosts, no more Christmas magic, and certainly no more faith in the words of a certain clumsy sea captain. The world suddenly seemed a much bleaker and colder place than it had ever been.

Her delicate features set in hard lines, she spun away from him. "Shouldn't you be preparing to return to your ship? I would not want to be the one responsible for you neglecting your duties."

"My duties be hanged. The papers are probably already being drawn up for my court-martial." Trent was keenly aware himself that he should already have been on his way to Portsmouth. But how? How could he ever just go and leave her in this fashion?

He continued, "My ship, the blasted navy, none of that matters just now. I suppose it doesn't even matter if you believe what I say. Whether you will it or no, Chloe Anne Waverly, you have my love.

When I am long gone from this place, I will have left my heart with you."

He reached out to stroke her hair, but she shrank away even from that feather-light touch. Despairing, he let his hand drop back to his side.

"Well, then," he said hoarsely, "I suppose it only remains to bid you farewell, my dear. God keep you."

Turning on his heel, he forced himself to walk away before he made a complete fool of himself and became unmanned entirely. But he had not taken many steps when he heard a deep sob escape her.

"Will!"

He spun about eagerly when she called his name. Such a cry would have had the power to draw him back from many leagues farther than the short distance he had traveled. He made his way to her side in two long strides.

Tears flowing down her cheeks, Chloe rested one hand against his chest, tried to speak but couldn't. Yet no words were needed. His own heart quite full, Will opened his arms, and she rushed into them. She buried her face against him, weeping down the front of his uniform while he pressed feverish kisses against the silky tangle of her curls.

"Everything is going to be all right, love, I promise you," he said. "I could not save Windhaven for you, but I swear I will build it up again."

"Th-that is too good of you, Will, but you c-cannot put back the memories." She sniffed. "All those times I spent with P-Papa in the parlor and . . . and my old room—"

"You can never lose all that, Chloe Anne. Those memories will always be a part of you. But if you will let me, I want to give you new ones, make Windhaven even grander than before."

"It can never be the same."

"But we can make it better."

"It could end up worse."

"But it *could* be better."

His stubborn insistence succeeded in coaxing a shaky laugh from her. She raised her head to look at him. Her eyes still shimmered with tears, but that dull look that had so frightened him was gone. It was definitely Chloe Anne's eyes that regarded him, shining with her own particular wistfulness, that boundless supply of hope.

"Did you really mean what you said about caring for me?" she whispered. "I . . . I know I adore you, but that is the sort of absurd thing I do, falling in love with someone so fast. You are far too sensible."

"Yes, I am," Trent agreed. "That is why I am about to do the most sensible thing I have ever done."

Cupping her chin, he slowly lowered his face to hers. Her eyes widened, but her lips parted, trembling with eagerness. Trent paused for a heartbeat, taking time to savor the moment before he bent to capture her lips, tasting of her sweetness for the very first time.

Lest he frighten her, he checked the turbulence of his own emotions, making the kiss as gentle as possible. When he drew back, Chloe gave a shuddering sigh.

"Oh, Will. I have never been kissed that way before. I . . . I quite like it. Could you possibly do it again?"

Nothing loath to comply, he pulled her even tighter into his embrace. Chloe flung her own arms about his neck, and this time their lips met in a kiss that was not so gentle, but filled with a passion that shook Trent to the core of his soul.

Fairly crushing her against him, he raised her off her feet, burying his face in her hair.

"Chloe Anne," he groaned. "We have so little time, my love. I cannot even stay to marry you."

"It doesn't matter," she murmured, her breath warm against his neck. "I'll wait for you to come back, Will. Even if it takes forever."

"It will seem like forever," he said, then broke off with an oath, sensing they were about to be intruded upon. Mr. Doughty stood at the entrance to the garden, twisting his hat in his hands. The steward did not look in the least surprised to find Chloe Anne in the captain's arms, but Trent eased her gently from him. She blushed deeply when she saw Doughty, the seaman giving her a wink and a grin.

"Beg pardon fer interruptin', Cap'n," Doughty said, wiping away his smile and coming to attention as he faced Will. "But the coachman, sir. He be wonderin' if he should unhitch the horses or if ye still mean to be leavin' soon."

Trent longed for nothing more than to send word for the carriage to be fetched back to the stables. He sighed deeply, tucking Chloe Anne's arm firmly within his.

"Tell the coachman I shall be ready in . . . in ten minutes."

"Very good, sir." Doughty gave a feeble imitation of a salute. "And I suppose you'll be wantin' to have me clapped in arms."

In truth, the problem Samuel Doughty posed was one Trent had given little thought to during the past harrowing hours. He regarded his steward now in frowning perplexity. "I certainly should. I still would like to know what the deuce brought you back here."

"I never actually left, Cap'n. I've been hiding out in the old cow barn all this time. I knew there would be a hue and cry after me, and I figured to just wait it out. I didn't think anyone would think to look for me here at Windhaven."

He had been right about that, Trent thought with a grudging admiration. Doughty always had been a most clever rogue.

"Then I realized the house was afire," Doughty concluded. "What else could I do but sound the alarm? Leastwise, I am powerful sorry for all the trouble I caused ye, Cap'n, and ready to take my punishment like a man."

No one looked more penitent than Samuel P. Doughty. Trent knew it was his duty to harden his heart against that woebegone face. But how could he also ignore the way Chloe Anne was tugging against his sleeve, making great pleading eyes at him?

Trent expelled his breath and swore. "Oh, get the devil out of here, Doughty."

"Sir?" The big man gaped at him.

"I never saw you come back," Trent said. "Now get going before I change my mind."

Chloe emitted a happy cry and tugged him down to plant a swift kiss upon his cheek, but Doughty, the great lumbering fool, just stood there shuffling his feet.

"If it's all the same to you, sir, I'd rather not desert. I've done a good deal of thinking about this. If you could somehow see your way clear to pardoning me, I would like another chance."

It was Trent's turn to stare.

Doughty scratched his chin in thoughtful fashion. "Smuggling just don't seem to have the same appeal it once did. And I'd be lucky to find any of me old mates still about after that last raid."

"But what about your dear, gray-haired old mum?" Chloe asked.

Doughty gave a sheepish grin. "Like as not, she'd break a gin bottle over my head if I was ever to turn up on her doorstep again. Besides, I been worrying about you, Cap'n."

"Me?" Trent said.

"Aye, what sort of scurvy knave would you end up with as yer new steward? One as would likely muck up the job of polishing your brass and not have the least notion how to disguise the taste of your salt pork when it's been sitting in the barrel too long."

"Very true," Trent said gravely. "He probably wouldn't know how to whistle me up a wind either."

"So if you would mind not hanging me this time, Cap'n, I'd be mighty grateful. Perhaps just a flogging or—"

"Whatever are you bothering me about, Mr. Doughty?" Trent growled. "By your own admission, you never left. Now be about your business and see that my things—whatever is left of them—have been bestowed aboard the carriage."

Chloe Anne gave Trent's arm a fierce hug. Doughty stared at him, and for a moment tears actually stood in the big man's eyes.

"Aye, aye, sir." He snapped off the smartest salute he had ever given. He lumbered off to do Trent's bidding, breaking into that familiar cheerful whistling.

Yet it was most strange. Trent found he had actually missed the irritating sound. He turned back to Chloe Anne, who was beaming up at him, brimful of pride and happiness.

But her smile faded with the consciousness of how little time remained to them. Trent would have drawn her into his arms, but she pulled away, knowing one thing remained that she had to do.

Skittering back to the bench, she searched the bushes frantically until she found her discarded statue of Saint Nicholas. Rushing back to Trent, she pressed it into his hands.

"Here," she said. "I want you to have this."

Trent glanced down at the statue and protested. "Nay, Chloe Anne. This is the last gift your father ever gave you. I could not possibly accept it."

"Oh yes, you must. I don't need it any longer, but you . . ." Chloe fought back a fresh influx of tears, willing herself not to think of all the dangers Will might face in the months ahead. "You will need the protection of Saint Nicholas more than I."

Trent pulled her back into his arms. "I will need nothing but the memory of your face, looking up at me this way. 'Tis enough to bring any sailor home from the sea." He bestowed upon her another fierce kiss, only breaking off to say anxiously, "You really will wait for me, Chloe Anne? Can you truly keep believing that no matter what, I will return to you?"

"Oh, Will," she said, smiling through her tears, reaching up to tenderly stroke his cheek, "keeping the faith is what I do best."

Epilogue

Christmas Eve, 1815

It seemed far too warm for Christmas. A most
gentle breeze sang through the rigging of the merchant vessel *Chloe Anne* where it rocked at anchor
near the harbor of Kingston, Jamaica.

The deck, normally bustling with activity, stood
quiet in the midafternoon sunshine, a calm fraught
with an air of expectancy, breathless waiting. Mrs.
William Trent experienced more difficulty than
usual in keeping her restless children from hanging over the side rail and tumbling into the blue
waters below.

Seated atop an empty rum barrel, Chloe balanced
baby Horatio on one knee, striving to think up yet
another tale to keep her older two offspring occupied. It was most difficult considering that they
knew Mr. Doughty would be returning from shore
at any moment in the longboat. Marie and young
Will took a great interest in the cargo he would
carry, which was sure to contain sweetmeats and
other mysteriously interesting packages.

In desperation, Chloe dredged up her statue of
Saint Nicholas to show them, although it was a
struggle to keep Horatio from stuffing it in his
mouth, which was where everything went these

days. Prying Saint Nicholas loose from those chubby little hands, Chloe told of the legend her father had woven for her on a Christmas Eve so long ago.

". . . And ever since the day Saint Nicholas gave each of those three young ladies a bag of gold, he has evermore been considered the protector of all maidens everywhere."

"And sailors, too. Doughty said so, Mama." Young Will leaned up against Chloe's knee, his blue eyes gone dreamy. The boy wholeheartedly embraced anything hinting of legend far more swiftly than he learned his alphabet.

"Yes, that is right, Willie," Chloe said.

But Marie, ever her papa's daughter, folded her arms across her chest. "Humph," she said with all the skepticism her five-year-old voice could muster. "I don't see how one man could do all that."

Flicking back one dark curl, she turned, preparing to consult that ultimate authority aboard the *Chloe Anne*. Captain Will Trent, late of His Majesty's Royal Navy, came strolling across the quarterdeck. Even without the glitter of his epaulets, Chloe thought fondly that her husband still presented quite the striking figure, more handsome than ever.

"Papa!" With a happy shout, young Will launched himself at Trent's legs. The captain took it in his stride, accustomed to withstanding this onslaught with as much aplomb as he balanced upon a pitching deck during a storm.

While Trent delighted his young son by scooping him up to perch high onto his shoulder, Marie faced her father, hands planted on her hips. "Captain! Mama has been telling us the most 'credible story."

"What is it this time?" Trent asked with an indulgent laugh.

"All 'bout this magic Nicholas person. That he takes care of sailors 'n' ladies 'n' everything. Do you believe such a thing can be true, Papa?"

He met Chloe's eyes over the children's heads. His mouth curved into that tender smile that ever had the power to make her heart stand still.

"Oh yes, Marie," he said huskily. "It is all quite true. Old Saint Nick performs his duties admirably well."